LAUGH AND LEARN

HUMOROUS AMERICAN SHORT STORIES

SECOND EDITION

Mira B. Felder ■ Anna Bryks Bromberg

 LONGMAN

Laugh and Learn: Humorous American Short Stories, second edition

Addison Wesley Longman, 10 Bank Street, White Plains, NY 10606-1951

Editorial Director: Joanne Dresner
Senior Acquisitions Editor: Allen Ascher
Development Editor: Randee Falk
Associate Editor: Jessica Miller
Production Editor: Karen Philippidis
Text Design: Christine Gehring-Wolf
Electronic Production Supervisor: Kim Teixeira
Composition: Kathleen Marks, Kim Teixeira
Cover design: Naomi Ganor
Cover art: George B. Kelly
Chapter opening illustrations: Gina Sample

Copyrights and Acknowledgements appear on page 163.

Library of Congress Cataloging–in–Publication Data
Felder, Mira B.
    Laugh and learn: a basic reader / Mira B. Felder, Anna Bryks Bromberg.
      p.   cm.
    ISBN 0–201–83414–6
    1. Readers—United States. 2. United States—Civilization—
    —Problems, exercises, etc. 3. English language—Textbooks for
    foreign speakers. I. Bromberg, Anna Bryks. II. Title.
PE 1127.H5F44 1996
428.6 ' 4—dc21   96–48206
                                        CIP

3 4 5 6 7 8 9 10 — CRS — 01 00 99 98

Contents

Preface

Laugh and Learn (second edition) is a thoroughly revised text which reflects the philosophical changes regarding the nature of reading and new perceptions of student reading needs. Using the interactive approach to reading, this text combines authentic, high-interest literature with pre-reading, reading, vocabulary, writing, discussion, and structure exercises. It is suitable for beginning students of English as a Second Language, as well as for high school and college students who do not speak and write standard English.

The selections in this book, which are unadapted and unabridged, are generously glossed and deal with aspects of everyday life. Thus, there are stories about breaking a habit, finding a job, getting along with one's neighbors, and writing thank-you notes. The accompanying exercises provide ample opportunity to practice these life skills. In addition, these exercises, which are thematically grouped, promote critical thinking. The pre-reading, comprehension, discussion, and inference questions provide further topic exploration, oral interaction, and opportunities for written reaction and self-expression.

There are many people we wish to thank at Addison Wesley Longman: Joanne Dresner, Editorial Director, for first introducing us to Addison Wesley Longman and making us feel welcome; Allen Ascher, Senior Acquisitions Editor, for his encouragement and suggestions and for always being there when we needed him; Randee Falk, Development Editor, for giving generously of her time and expertise; Jessica Miller, Associate Editor, for being responsive to our suggestions; Karen Philippidis, Assistant Production Editor, and Kim Teixeira, Electronic Production Supervisor, for expertly scrutinizing every detail of the text; Anne Boynton-Trigg, Marketing Manager; Victoria Denkus, Senior Marketing Associate; Elizabeth Barker, Marketing Assistant; and Jennifer Morgan, Sales Representative, for their enthusiastic help; and Amy Durfy, Senior Administrative Assistant, for ensuring that the follow-up was complete. Our thanks also go to Marina Zilberman, who patiently typed portions of the text.

No book gets written without a great deal of assistance from family and friends. We are especially grateful to our children, Joseph, Jenny, and Aaron Felder; Suri, Robi, and Esti Flegmann; and Brian and Benjamin Bromberg, who gave of themselves and their computers whenever asked. Special thanks go to Simon Felder, expert proofreader, for his patience in the face of missed appointments and broken social engagements.

Introduction

Laugh and Learn is an anthology of humorous stories and essays that will give students a glimpse of American life and American idioms. Each selection is preceded by an illustration and pre-reading questions and is followed by post-reading exercises which include comprehension and inference questions, vocabulary and idiom exercises, and writing and discussion questions, in addition to a variety of structure exercises. We thus provide the student with many opportunities to interact with the text in order to achieve better comprehension and mastery of English grammatical structures.

The ten units contain exercises that highlight the material to be mastered. Verb exercises are arranged in order of difficulty and build on each other as the text progresses. Therefore, if the selections are not being studied in sequence, we recommend that the instructor skip a story occasionally but not go back and forth in the text. Furthermore, the selections work from fairly simple to more-complex sentence structures, so some orderly sequence is necessary. Basically, though, units can be used independently to fit instructor preferences or student needs.

Vocabulary

All words and phrases not easily understood from their context are defined in each selection, even though they may have appeared and been glossed previously. If there are multiple meanings for any word or expression, we have provided them, with the first definition a synonym for the word as it is used in the text so that the student can usually make a direct substitution of the definition for the word being defined.

We use two methods for defining the vocabulary and idioms: (1) New or difficult words are marked in the text by a number and are defined in the margin and (2) idioms and phrases are indicated by an asterisk (*) and are defined in a list at the end of the story. Students should review that list before beginning to read each selection. The illustrations accompanying the selections also aid in illuminating the sense of each piece.

Exercises

The exercises, which are short and varied, are designed to maximize student participation. They call not only for standard fill-in and substitution-type answers but also for the student to participate in role playing and to generate his/her own sentences.

Previewing the Story This exercise asks the student to make predictions about the literary selection and thus set his/her own goals for reading.

Thinking about the Topic These questions tap into the prior knowledge and cultural schemata of the reader so that the student can relate personally and culturally to the events in the story.

Comprehension These questions review student understanding of the main idea and details of the story.

Responding to the Story Inferential questions test for attention to nuance. The student must always respond in complete sentences, orally or in writing; a simple yes or no is not sufficient. Also included are questions regarding cultural differences and personal reactions and assessments.

Vocabulary Because word and phrase acquisition has the greatest priority for a language student, varied vocabulary exercises appear after each selection to help reinforce the use of new words and expressions. Vocabulary exercises include fill-in, substitution, and dictionary exercises—both in and out of sentence context. Idiom exercises give students an opportunity to generate original sentences, following the example of a particular idiomatic structure.

Articles, Prepositions, and Word Forms One problem common to students of the English language is mastering the correct use of articles, prepositions, and word endings. To this end, we have included many exercises that address this problem throughout the text, and we suggest that students read each completed sentence aloud in order to become accustomed to the correct usage.

Verbs The verb exercises deal with a wide range of skills, from knowing the simple past tense of regular verbs to composing complete structures, such as the continuous and perfect tenses, from a model. The exercises test many different aspects of verb competence, including subject-verb agreement, regular and irregular endings, and the correct use of active and passive voice, imperatives, infinitives, and gerunds.

Sentence Structure Most selections are followed by at least one structure, exercise, or pattern drill. These exercises range from using proper word order in a sentence to combining sentences by choosing the correct coordinating conjunctions.

Other Exercises Many of the readings contain instances of particular grammatical or structural points that require elaboration and further study. These points are dealt with in exercises that treat such topics as contractions, *there is/there are, some/any, to make/to do,* punctuation, spelling, pronunciation, adjectives and adverbs, superlatives and comparatives, and quotations.

Topics for Discussion Every group of exercises contains suggestions for discussion. Although generated by the selections, they are also used for more general assignments drawing on student experiences.

Topics for Writing Writing assignments reinforce many of the reading comprehension skills such as comparing / contrasting, visualizing, and summarizing. They often require the use of the vocabulary and grammatical structures which were previously taught. Students are asked to share writing with the rest of the class, thus promoting peer learning.

Special Activities These exercises engage students in practical, real-life situations suggested by the readings; they include writing letters, filling out a job application, reading drug labels and want ads, and role-playing. They call for the application of language skills developed in other lessons throughout the text.

Answer Key

For easy reference, an Answer Key is provided at the end of the book. The Answer Key enables the instructor to assign independent work (such as a specific grammatical exercise for review or reinforcement), knowing that the student can check his or her own answers and make corrections where necessary.

Thank You, Uncle Ben, for the Nicest Whatever-It-Is That Ever Ruined a House —MAGGIE GRANT

Thank You, Uncle Ben, for the Nicest Whatever-It-Is That Ever Ruined a House

◆ PREVIEWING THE STORY

Look at the picture, the title, and the first paragraph of the story. Answer the questions, explaining each answer.

1. What do you think the woman in the picture is doing?

2. What might she be thinking about?

3. What might the object in the picture be used for?

4. What do you think the story is about?

◆ THINKING ABOUT THE TOPIC

Think about and answer the following questions.

1. Think of a country other than the United States. On what occasions do people give presents?

2. How do people thank others for giving them presents?

3. What do you do with a present you don't need or like?

I usually manage to finish writing my Christmas thank-you notes by Jan. 31 at worst,* but this year I've bogged down on* Uncle Ben. That's my rich uncle, the one who's going to leave me a nice legacy[1] if I survive him.* Which seems doubtful[2] at the moment.

[1] gift
[2] unsure, uncertain

There is also this about Uncle Ben: he's the type who would cut a person out of his will* if that person failed to thank him for a Christmas present, or even failed to be adequately[3] enthusiastic[4] about it. My problem this year is that—well, just glance at these unfinished notes and perhaps you'll understand.

[3] enough
[4] excited

December 28

Dear Uncle Ben,

We had a lovely Christmas with all sorts of exciting presents, particularly[5] yours. At first we were puzzled[6] about its use, since no instruction sheet* was enclosed, but suddenly light dawned*—an electric bean pot, what a marvelous[7] idea! To be able to plug in and bake old-fashioned beans right at the table is such an innovation[8] we've invited a few friends in to participate in your gift's debut[9]! At this very moment the feast[10] is hissing away* in the dining room and . . .

[5] especially
[6] confused
[7] wonderful
[8] new idea
[9] first appearance
[10] large meal

January 3

Dear Uncle Ben,

I know you'll be amused to learn that when we opened your present we jumped to the conclusion* it was a bean pot. We realized the error of our ways* when some beans we were cooking exploded[11] all over the dining room. The pattern[12] they made on the ceiling looked exactly like Santa Claus and his eight tiny reindeer! Fortunately our insurance covers the cost of repainting the room and repairing the chandelier.[13]

[11] burst with a loud noise
[12] picture or design

[13] fancy hanging lamp

Now our neighbor has told us your present is actually a bed-warmer and we're pleased as punch* because both John and I suffer from cold feet these winter nights and as a matter of fact he is now snoring peacefully abed with the warmer toasting his . . .

January 5

Dear Uncle Ben,

Excuse the scribble,[14] but I'm writing this in my lap so I can stay close to John's bed in case he needs anything. He's under sedation* after burning both his feet (I won't bother you with the details of how it happened) but will soon be able to get about* on crutches. Luckily a personal injury clause* in our insurance policy* will pay his salary while he's off work.

I must delay no longer in thanking you for the lovely humidifier;[15] it was so generous of you. About an hour ago I set it going in the living room and already . . .

January 20

Dear Uncle Ben,

At last a peaceful moment to write you! We've been higgledy-piggledy lately due to the living room broadloom[16] having to be torn up and taken away to be dyed. It got badly stained in a foolish little mishap[17] we had with steam and boiling water and my Sheraton table had to be refinished. But it's an ill wind,* etc., because I love the rug's new color and insurance paid for everything.

Now to business! We are simply delighted with your Christmas present though I'm going to confess that at first we were unsure about its function.[18] Then John's office manager dropped in and told us it's an outdoor barbecue.[19] How silly of us not to realize it at once! To celebrate the new look in the living room we're going to prepare dinner there tonight, with John acting as chef. As I write he is fussing around* with steaks and things . . .

[14] fast and messy writing

[15] machine that adds water to the air

[16] carpet

[17] accident

[18] use

[19] grill

January 31

Dear Uncle Ben,

    As you can see by this letterhead,[20] we are staying at a hotel. We had a fire at the house, but don't be alarmed, it wasn't too bad, mostly smoke damage. A marvelous cleaning crew[21] is at work, busily washing walls, shampooing furniture and so forth. I understand this is a frightfully[22] costly operation so thank goodness we were covered by insurance. In connection with this, I am expecting the company's adjuster[23] to call at any moment, but meanwhile am dashing this off* to thank you for . . .

[20] name and address on a piece of paper

[21] workers

[22] very

[23] insurance company employee

February 1

Dear Uncle Ben,

    If a Mr. Smither, an insurance adjuster, should try to get in touch with you in any way, I do beg you to disregard[24] him—I'm afraid he's mentally ill. He called in to see me about some claims[25] we've had recently and suddenly started screaming and shouting dreadful[26] things about the lovely Christmas present you sent us. Well, really! No man in his right mind would act that way about an inanimate[27] object! The only thing to do is ignore[28] him. And now, my darling uncle, I hope you are going to forgive the long delay in writing to thank you for the . . . for the . . . ◆

[24] pay no attention to

[25] money requested from an insurance company for damages

[26] terrible

[27] not alive

[28] pay no attention to

IDIOMS AND PHRASES*

at worst	*under poorest conditions*
bogged down on	*stuck on*
survive him	*live longer than he*
to cut out of his will	*to leave nothing (to someone) at death*
instruction sheet	*directions explaining how to use something*
light dawned (on someone)	*(someone) understood*
hissing away	*making sharp, whistling noises*
jumped to a conclusion	*decided too quickly or without thinking*
error of our ways	*our mistake*
pleased as punch	*very pleased*
under sedation	*made sleepy with a drug*
get about	*move around*
personal injury clause	*the part of an insurance policy that deals with getting hurt in the home*

(Continued on next page)

insurance policy   *a contract giving protection against damage or loss*

ill wind   *"It's an ill wind that blows nobody any good." A proverb: No matter how bad a happening is, someone can usually gain something from it.*

fussing around   *performing unnecessary activities*

dashing (something) off   *doing (something) quickly*

POST-READING

Comprehension

1. Why is the narrator (the person telling the story) trying to write Uncle Ben a letter?

2. Why doesn't she know how to use the gift?

3. Why is it so important to her to find a use for this gift?

4. Describe three uses she and her husband make of the gift.

5. How many thank-you notes did she begin to write?

6. List three accidents caused by using the gift.

7. What kind of repairs had to be done in the house as a result of the gift?

8. Who paid for the repairs? Why?

Responding to the Story

1. How do you think the narrator really feels about all the accidents that were caused by using this gift?

2. Put yourself in the narrator's place. How would you handle her situation?

3. How does Mr. Smither, the insurance adjuster, feel about the gift? How can you tell?

4. If you were Mr. Smither, how would you handle this case? Would you advise your company to pay for the damage?

5. The narrator never figures out what the gift is for. What do you think it might be for?

6. Do you think that Uncle Ben wanted the gift to be confusing to his niece? Explain your answer.

VOCABULARY

Vocabulary Builder

Replace the underlined word in each sentence with the proper synonym from the list.

enough	large meal
excited	design
kinds	use
especially	pay no attention to
confused	terrible
wonderful	accident

1. We <u>particularly</u> liked your present.

2. We were <u>enthusiastic</u> about it as soon as we saw it.

3. It's so wonderful that I'm not sure I can thank you <u>adequately</u> for it.

4. Even though we are delighted with your present, we are unsure of its <u>function</u>.

5. After trying to use the gift in several ways, we are still very <u>puzzled</u> about it.

6. At first we thought it was an electric bean pot, which seemed like a <u>marvelous</u> idea.

7. We thought we would have a <u>feast</u> and serve old-fashioned baked beans.

8. However, the beans exploded and formed a funny <u>pattern</u> on the ceiling.

9. When we tried to use your gift as a humidifier, it caused <u>dreadful</u> damage to the carpet.

10. As a result of that little <u>mishap</u>, we also had to refinish the table.

11. If the insurance adjuster calls, the only thing to do is <u>ignore</u> him.

Idiom Exercise

Exercise 1

Complete the following sentences by using the idioms listed.

> jump to the conclusion
> survive him
> at worst
> cut me out of his will

1. If I ask him what the present is, will he _____ that I don't like it?

2. _____, he will _____ if I don't thank him.

3. However, if I use his present without knowing what it is, I may not _____.

Exercise 2

Using away *with a present participle (verb + -ing) indicates doing something continuously or repeatedly. Write five sentences using any five of the following phrases.*

> hissing away   screaming away
> coughing away   dancing away
> sneezing away   yelling away
> talking away

EXAMPLE: I tried to get her attention, but she was talking away on the telephone and didn't notice me.

Say It Right

How many of these words can you pronounce correctly? Try them and see.

1. broadloom   BRAWD-loom
2. humidifier   hyoo MID i fai er
3. debut   DAY byu
4. adequately   AD i kwit lee
5. chandelier   shand di LEER
6. inanimate   in AN i mit
7. barbecue   BAHR bi kyoo

Vocabulary: The Home

Kitchen
cabinet
sink
refrigerator
oven
stove

Bathroom
shower
toilet
bathtub
sink

Living Room
sofa
coffee table
rug
television set
lamp
bookcase

Bedroom
bed
dresser
chest
night table
mirror
closet

Dining Room
chandelier
table
chair
buffet

Porch
lawn chair
barbecue
umbrella

Exercise 1

ROLE PLAY: Pretend that you own the house in the drawing and that there has been an accident. You want to file a claim for damage in your home. Your partner is the insurance adjuster. Describe to him or her what items were damaged, where those items are found in your home, and how the accident happened. You may use the drawing to help you. When you are finished, switch roles.

(Continued on next page)

Exercise 2

Describe to your partner what your own house or apartment looks like and what furniture you have in each room.

Exercise 3

Pretend you are looking for a new apartment or house. How would you look for one? What would you look for?

Word Forms

Fill in the correct word form from those listed. Each form should be used, and some forms should be used twice.

1. act, actor, actions, acting
   a. Which _____ could play the part of Uncle Ben?
   b. Did John _____ nervous when you saw him?
   c. The insurance adjuster was _____ strange.
   d. _____ speak louder than words.

2. invite, invitation, inviting
   a. Please _____ him to the outdoor barbecue.
   b. Don't wait for an _____.
   c. We are _____ a few friends for dinner.
   d. The feast looks _____.

3. manage, manager, managing, management
   a. Can you _____ to deliver the rug tomorrow?
   b. John's office _____ is very helpful.
   c. The adjuster's _____ of the claim made Maggie unhappy.
   d. How is John _____ to go to work on crutches?

4. celebrate, celebrity, celebrating, celebration
   a. We were _____ Christmas by exchanging gifts.
   b. When I get my insurance money, I am going to _____ by throwing a party.
   c. Uncle Ben was a _____ in our family.
   d. We held a big _____ on New Year's Day.

5. amuse, amusing, amusement
   a. When John was home after the accident, I had to find ways to _____ him.
   b. His gift was _____.
   c. The insurance adjuster did not greet us with _____.
   d. Are you _____ yourself?

Verb Tenses: Simple Present and Past

Exercise 1

Stories are usually told mainly in the past tense. Read the following paragraph, which uses the present tense. Underline the verbs in the simple present. Then rewrite the story, putting each present tense verb into the simple past. Some of the past tense forms are irregular.

Every few days this month, I write another letter to Uncle Ben. But I never finish or mail these letters. I want to thank Uncle Ben for his Christmas present. But what is his present? I have no idea. I know one thing about this present: it is dangerous. Mr. Smither, the insurance adjuster, agrees with this. I know what the present isn't: it isn't a bean pot, a bed-warmer, a humidifier, or a barbecue. I show Uncle Ben's present to friends and ask them what it is, but no one seems to know. I hope Uncle Ben isn't angry at me!

Tell a partner the story of an interesting present you gave or received. Use past tense verbs to tell the story.

Exercise 2

Fill in the blank with the correct form of the verb in parentheses. Use only the simple present or past tense.

Maggie _____ to the store and _____
           (go)   (buy)
John a present. She _____ it to him by mail. After he
                (send)
_____ it, he _____ her a thank-you letter.
  (receive)   (write)
When she _____ it, she _____ that he
         (open)   (realize)
was thanking her for the wrong present. Obviously, John
_____ mixed up. Maggie _____ to tell
   (be)   (want)
John about the mistake, but she _____ afraid to embarrass
                         (be)
him.

The next day, Maggie _____ to prepare a birthday
                   (decide)
dinner for John. She _____ a big pot of chicken and rice.
            (make)

(Continued on next page)

The telephone _____, and she _____
              (ring)   (forget)

the food. It _____ and _____. Maggie
              (burn)   (explode)

_____ from the noise.
    (jump)

    When John _____ to her house, she said, "I
                        (come)

_____ sorry. You _____ which gift I
    (be)   (forget)

_____ you, and I _____ that I was
    (give)   (forget)

cooking for your birthday."

Identifying Subjects and Verbs

Underline the subject (noun or pronoun only) and circle the verb in each of the following sentences. (One of the sentences has two subjects and two verbs.)

1. We had a lovely party.
2. We received all sorts of exciting and different presents.
3. However, your present was the most puzzling.
4. Suddenly, light dawned—it was an electric bean pot.
5. Now, we can bake old-fashioned beans right at the table.
6. We invited a few friends in for dinner.
7. At this very minute, the feast is hissing away in the dining room.
8. What caused that loud noise?
9. It is an explosion!
10. Is this really a bean pot?

Word Order: Statements

Arrange the following groups of words in customary word order to make complete statements.

tired
is
she   Example: She is very tired today.
very
today

1. managed
   finish
   I
   letter
   to
   my

2. lovely
   Uncle Ben
   gift
   sent
   a

3. friends
   often
   my
   visit
   to
   come

4. very
   pattern
   this
   interesting
   is
   the
   ceiling
   on

5. insurance
   repainting
   cost
   room
   our
   the
   of
   covers
   the

6. John
   carpet
   living room
   the
   the
   cleaned
   in

7. nice
   letter
   write
   a
   I
   should
   thank-you

8. decided
   table
   to
   I
   refinish
   the

9. unhappy
   seemed
   something
   she
   about
   very

10. gift
    he
    relative
    each
    gave
    a

Simple Present and Present Continuous

The present continuous tense is formed with the present tense of the verb *to be* and the present participle (*-ing* form) of the main verb. The present continuous is used to talk about something that is happening at the present moment. The simple present tense, on the other hand, is used to talk about things that happen repeatedly (for example, habits and routines). Non-action verbs, like *be, know, seem,* and *like,* occur just in the simple present; they do not occur in the present continuous.

(Continued on next page)

Complete the sentences with the verbs in parentheses. Use either the simple present tense or the present continuous.

EXAMPLE: This year I _____*am having*_____ trouble finishing my
                   (have)
Christmas thank-you notes.

1. I usually _____ to finish writing my Christmas
              (manage)
   thank-you notes on time.

2. Uncle Ben _____ the type who would cut a person
              (be)
   out of his will.

3. At this very moment, the feast _____ away in
               (hiss)
   the dining room.

4. Our insurance policy _____ any damages that
              (cover)
   occur in the home because of accidents.

5. Both John and I _____ from cold feet every winter.
              (suffer)

6. But now John _____ peacefully.
              (snore)

7. Excuse the scribble, but I _____ this letter in my
              (write)
   lap.

8. John _____ under sedation.
              (be)

9. I _____ the rug's new color.
              (love)

10. As you can see by this letterhead, we _____ at
                   (stay)
    a hotel.

11. A marvelous cleaning crew _____ the walls and
                   (wash)
    _____ the furniture now.
  (shampoo)

12. Right now, I _____ for the adjuster and
             (wait)
    _____ this off to thank you.
  (dash)

*F*OLLOW UP

Topics for Discussion

1. This story ends with another unfinished letter. What do you think might happen next? Do you think the narrator ever sends a letter to Uncle Ben?

2. From the thank-you notes, what do you think the gift looks like? Draw a picture of the gift, and explain the drawing to the class. (Your drawing should not look like the one on page 1).

3. Did you ever receive a gift you didn't like? What was it and what did you do with it? Did you have to make excuses to the person who gave it to you for not using it? If so, what excuses did you make?

4. If you could choose, what present would you like to receive?

5. How do you decide what kind of gift to buy for a friend or a relative? Do you find such decisions easy or difficult to make?

6. Did you ever give a gift that you later thought was not a good gift for the person you gave it to? If so, what was it and why wasn't it a good gift?

7. Was a house that you lived in ever damaged? If so, what happened?

8. In your city or state, what is the usual way of insuring your property?

Topics for Writing

1. There are many occasions when one needs to write a thank-you note. Write thank-you notes for two of the following:

   1. wedding gift
   2. graduation gift
   3. baby present
   4. birthday present
   5. house gift
   6. anniversary present
   7. Christmas present

   In each letter, mention the gift you received and describe how you will use it. Be sure to include a salutation, a closing, and your signature.

2. In a two-paragraph essay, describe the most unusual gift you've ever received.

(Continued on next page)

3. Invent an object that could be an unusual but useful household gift. On one side of a piece of paper, describe what the object looks like and, if possible, draw a picture of it. On the other side, tell what it does. Read the description to your classmates and show them the picture. See if the other students can guess what the gift would be used for. Would they like to receive this gift?

4. Write a three-paragraph essay telling what you consider to be the three most useful household gifts and explaining why these gifts are so useful. Or write your essay on three common household gifts that are not useful.

5. Write a dialogue between John and his wife after he used the present as a bed-warmer and burned both his feet. How do they each feel about Uncle Ben and his gift?

6. Pretend that you are Uncle Ben. It's February, and you haven't received a thank-you letter from your niece. What is your reaction? Write her a letter, telling her what you think.

7. Do you have a relative you try to please? In a three-paragraph essay, describe this person and why you try to please him/her.

8. Write a short story in which a person tries to please a rich relative. Does this person come to a bad end or live happily ever after?

Diary of a Quitter

—Ralph Reppert

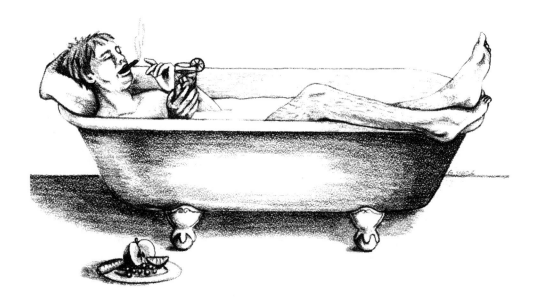

Diary of a Quitter

◆ **PREVIEWING THE STORY**

Look at the picture, the title, and the first paragraph of the story. Answer the questions, explaining each answer.

1. What is a diary?

2. What is this man trying to quit?

3. What do you think the story is about?

4. What do you think the bathtub has to do with quitting?

◆ **THINKING ABOUT THE TOPIC**

Think about and answer the following questions.

1. Some people feel that if they stop smoking, they will gain weight. What is the connection?

2. What are some of the things that people experience when they try to give up smoking? How do they feel?

3. Is it easy to give up smoking? Why or why not?

4. In your city or state, are there any rules about smoking in restaurants, trains, theaters, or offices? What are these rules?

Sunday. Too much party last night and so a cigarette hangover[1] today. Even my blood hurts. I think I will break the smoking habit.[2]

Monday. Come on, willpower!* I keep saying to myself, "I don't *want* a cigarette!" And deep within me a small voice keeps answering, "The heck you don't!"*

Tuesday. This is supposed to be my edgy[3] day, but I'm fine. Sharp. Alert.[4] I never noticed before how much noise our cat makes stomping[5] around the house.

I guess I won't have a highball.[6] Alcohol makes you want to smoke. My wife Harriet suggests a warm bath to soothe[7] my nerves.

Wednesday. My neighbor George Peebles quits smoking every month or so. He says to eat fruit and lay off* starches and fats, because kicking the cigarette habit* makes a man put on weight.

Breakfast today: sliced apple, quartered orange, eight grapes, raw carrot. And another warm bath.

Thursday. I knew my sliced apple, quartered orange, eight grapes, and raw carrot for breakfast reminded me of something. It's what they give the monkeys at the zoo.

Most people who quit smoking get irritable[8] on the fourth day, but not me. My abstinence[9] has nothing to do with the things I said today. I've *always* hated broccoli and dog acts on TV.

Another warm bath. I lay in the tub and notice how badly the bathroom needs painting.

I have given up TV. It makes me thirsty for a highball and highballs make me want to smoke.

Friday. I can honestly say that quitting cigarettes is as easy as taking candy from a baby.* (Did you ever try taking candy from a baby?)

My sense of smell, which flew the coop* when I began smoking years ago, has come home to roost.* Today I took Aunt Garnet to the station, put her on the train for Wilkes-Barre, and kissed her good-bye. Aunt Garnet smokes. It was like kissing Rocky Colavito.[10]

My taste buds,* deadened by years of smoking, have begun to flex[11] their little muscles again. I can taste toothpaste. I can't stand it.

Saturday. Two warm baths today. My fingers are wrinkled like prunes.

Another monkey breakfast. I have forgotten how to use a fork.

[1] unpleasant feeling after heavy use (usually of alcohol)
[2] an act repeated often
[3] nervous
[4] quick in thought or action
[5] stepping hard
[6] alcoholic drink
[7] make calm or quiet
[8] easily made nervous or angry
[9] staying away from
[10] a baseball player
[11] bend or stretch

I have given up running errands* for my wife. Running errands makes me want to watch TV, which makes me want a highball, which makes me want to smoke.

If there is one thing I am *not*, it's a man like my uncle Louis. When he quit drinking he went around knocking highballs out of people's hands. I see other people smoking. I don't try to influence them. I don't try to scare[12] them. I don't pity them. I envy them.

[12] frighten

Sunday. I cannot look another apple, orange, grape, or raw carrot in the face. Coffee for breakfast.

Another warm bath. Discovered something interesting: warm baths make me want to smoke. So do cold baths. So does going without a bath.

I've saved some money. No cigarettes for a week—two packs a day at 30¢ a pack—that's $4.20.

[13] sudden movement

[14] light on the back of a car

Backed out* of the garage and, in a nervous twitch[13] that never happened before, broke a taillight.[14] The man at the filling station* has ordered me a new one. For $4.20.

[15] ruler; person who controls

After a week without smoking I feel I am the captain of my soul, the master[15] of my fate. While feeling so masterful, have decided I *want* to smoke.

[16] person who is not brave

Took a warm bath. Mixed a stiff highball. Lit a cigarette. I am the cleanest coward[16] in Baltimore. ◆

IDIOMS AND PHRASES*

willpower	*the ability to control oneself and one's desires*
The heck you don't!	*an expression of disbelief*
lay off	*stay away from; not have or do*
kicking a habit	*make oneself stop doing something that one usually does but doesn't want to do*
as easy as taking candy from a baby	*very easy*
flew the coop	*went away*
come home to roost	*has come back*
taste buds	*the spots on the tongue that allow us to taste*
run errands	*go out to do small jobs for oneself or another person*
backed out	*walked or drove backwards*
filling station	*gasoline station*

POST-READING

Comprehension

1. Why did the narrator want to break his cigarette habit?

2. What did he eat for breakfast after he gave up smoking? Why did he eat this? What did it remind him of?

3. Why did he take so many baths?

4. Why did the narrator give up watching television? Why, later on, did he give up running errands for his wife?

5. What happened to his senses of smell and taste after he gave up smoking? How did he feel about these changes?

6. How is the narrator unlike his uncle Louis?

7. Why, according to the narrator, didn't he save any money after a week of not buying cigarettes?

8. What happened at the end of the week and the story?

Responding to the Story

1. On Tuesday, the narrator says that he is not edgy. Is he telling the truth? How can you tell?

2. In what ways does he show that, despite what he says, breaking the smoking habit is very difficult for him?

3. Why, at the end of the story, does he refer to himself as the "cleanest coward in Baltimore"?

4. Why do you think the narrator does not mention the health risks of smoking?

5. As you read the story, did you expect the narrator to succeed in quitting? Do you think he expected to succeed? How seriously did he try to quit smoking?

6. The story is called "Diary of a Quitter." After reading the story, what do you think "quitter" in the title might mean?

7. What else could the narrator have done to break this habit?

VOCABULARY

Vocabulary Builder

Fill in each blank with a word from the list.

habits	alert	soothe	abstinence	coward
hangover	quitter	irritable	taste buds	willpower

1. People who have had a lot to drink should not drive because alcohol makes people less _____.
2. Alcohol can also cause a person to wake up the next morning with a _____.
3. For reasons like these, some people decide the best solution is complete _____ from alcohol.
4. Smoking can have the effect of dulling people's _____ so that they don't appreciate good food as much.
5. Old _____ can be very hard to give up.
6. Smokers sometimes become very _____ when they try to give up smoking.
7. A warm bath is a good way to _____ one's nerves.
8. If you stop trying, you are being a _____.
9. The narrator felt he was a _____ because in the end he didn't have the courage to quit smoking.
10. To quit smoking, you need a lot of _____.

Meanings of *So*

Exercise 1

Match the meanings of so *with their use in the sentences.*

a. also

b. approximately, more or less

c. therefore, for this reason

d. very

___ 1. I smoked too much last night, so I have a cigarette hangover today.

___ 2. Warm baths make me want to smoke. So do cold baths.

___ 3. While feeling so masterful, I have decided I want to smoke.

___ 4. George Peebles quits smoking every month or so.

Exercise 2

Write four sentences of your own, one for each use of so.

Idiom Exercise

Rewrite each sentence below, replacing the underlined words with one of the idioms from the list.

> break the habit (of)   come home to roost
> kick the habit (of)   lay off
> flew the coop

1. <u>Stay away from</u> cigarettes if you want to stay healthy.
2. I can't <u>stop</u> smoking.
3. My willpower <u>ran away</u> when I tried to break the smoking habit.
4. Most people eat more when they <u>stop</u> smoking.
5. If you are not careful, your bad habits will <u>return</u>.

Word Forms

Fill in the correct word form from those listed. Each form should be used, and some forms should be used twice.

1. irritate, irritating, irritation, irritable
   a. I find it _____ when the cat stomps around
   the house.
   b. Cigarette smoke can _____ your eyes.
   c. Many people become _____ when they try to
   stop smoking.
   d. It is very _____ to watch dog acts on TV.
   e. Taking too many baths causes a skin _____.

2. hate, hating, hateful, hatred
   a. I _____ eating broccoli.
   b. _____ every bite of it, I ate my apple.
   c. Smoking in front of someone who is trying to quit is
   _____ behavior.
   d. _____ is a strong and destructive emotion.

(Continued on next page)

3. begin, began, beginner, beginning
   a. Let us _____ to kick the cigarette habit.
   b. He _____ to grow irritable on Tuesday.
   c. When it came to quitting smoking, he was just a
      _____.
   d. He is _____ to grow tired of his diet.

4. suggest, suggested, suggesting, suggestion
   a. What do you _____ I eat?
   b. The narrator found Mr. Peebles's _____ very helpful.
   c. What are you _____?
   d. His wife _____ that he take warm baths.

5. master, mastering, mastered, masterful
   a. I am the _____ of my fate.
   b. He still had not _____ his cigarette habit.
   c. Instead of being _____, the narrator was cowardly.
   d. _____ my cigarette habit is difficult.

S*TRUCTURE*

Adjectives and Adverbs

Adjectives modify, or give more information about, nouns. Adverbs modify, or give more information about, verbs (and adjectives). For example, the adjective *happy* gives more information about the noun *the child* in the sentence *She was a happy child* or the pronoun *she* in *She was happy*. The adverb *happily* gives more information about the verb *laughed* in the sentence *She laughed happily*.

Often, adverbs can be formed by adding *-ly* to an adjective. Sometimes when adverbs are formed this way, it is necessary to make spelling changes. For example:

happ*y* —> happ*i*ly
comfortab*le* —> comfortab*ly*

Exercise 1

Change the following adjectives to adverbs, correcting the spelling as necessary.

EXAMPLE: stiff   **stiffly**

1. bad   6. warm
2. honest   7. cold
3. easy   8. irritable
4. alert   9. sharp
5. edgy   10. nervous

Exercise 2

Fill in each blank with the adjective in parentheses or the adverb that is formed from that adjective.

EXAMPLE: He looked _____*irritably*_____ at the cat.
                              (irritable)

1. After smoking many cigarettes, he woke up with a

   _____ headache.
          (bad)

2. He decided that this time he would make an

   _____ effort to quit smoking.
        (honest)

3. He knew that quitting isn't _____.
                            (easy)

4. But he felt that this time he could do it _____.
                                    (easy)

5. On his first day without cigarettes, he had a wonderful,

   _____ feeling.
         (alert)

6. By the second day, he _____ wanted a cigarette.
                          (bad)

7. He was very _____.
                (nervous)

8. Taking a _____ bath didn't help.
           (warm)

9. He spoke _____ to his wife.
             (irritable)

10. He hated being so _____ all the time.
                (edgy)

11. He _____ decided that for him quitting wasn't
          (quick)
    worth it, so he lit another cigarette.

Exercise 3

Adjectives and adverbs can make a story more interesting by giving readers a clearer picture with more details. With a partner, write a short story, using as many adjectives and adverbs as you can. Look at the lists for some ideas. Read your story to the class.

ADJECTIVES

bad	big	cold
dark	difficult	easy
friendly/unfriendly	good	happy/unhappy
hot	hungry	irritable
interesting	nice	old
red (and other colors)	sad	small
tired	young	

ADVERBS

angrily	badly	carefully
happily	loudly	quickly
quietly	slowly	well

EXAMPLE: It was a cold, dark night. The small boy walked slowly down the road. He was tired and hungry. . . .

Exercise 4

Fill in the appropriate adjective or adverb in each blank below. Some blanks have more than one correct answer.

long	irritable	nervous
edgy	badly	new
sharp	honestly	stiff
alert	interesting	clean
warm	cold	

Yesterday, I heard a(n) _____ story. It was about a student named Norberto who was touring the United States of America by bus. On one of his tours, he sat next to a(n) _____ young man who smoked many cigarettes. This made Norberto _____ and _____. Norberto asked his neighbor to please stop smoking. His neighbor replied, "I _____ didn't know how my smoking affected you. I shall stop so that you can breathe _____ air."

Norberto was so impressed by the young man's kindness that he invited him for lunch. Their friendship lasted a _____ time.

Prepositions

Exercise 1

Complete the following sentences with the correct preposition.

on   in   to   for   of   from

EXAMPLE: <u>*On*</u> Monday I quit smoking.

1. Quitting cigarettes is as easy as taking candy _____ a baby.
2. I had an apple, an orange, some grapes, and a carrot _____ breakfast.
3. It reminded me _____ the food they give monkeys.
4. I've always hated broccoli and dog acts _____ TV.
5. I lay _____ the tub and noticed that the bathroom needs painting.
6. I took Aunt Garnet _____ the station and put her _____ the train that was going _____ Wilkes-Barre.
7. I've given up running errands _____ my wife.
8. I backed out _____ the garage.
9. I feel I am the master _____ my fate.
10. I am the cleanest coward _____ Baltimore.

Exercise 2

Use each of the prepositions above in a sentence of your own.

Some/Any

Some and *any* mean "a certain quantity" and are used before plural or uncountable nouns. *Some* is used in affirmative statements. *Any* is used in negative sentences or questions. However, when the question is really an invitation or a request, *some* is used.

Change each of the following sentences to a negative form.

EXAMPLE: The narrator wants to buy some cigarettes. (affirmative form)
The narrator doesn't want to buy any cigarettes. (negative form)

1. I ate some sliced apples and quartered oranges for breakfast this morning.
2. The narrator wants to eat some broccoli.
3. He saved some money last year when he stopped smoking.
4. The quitter put on some weight this month.
5. Uncle Louis wanted to knock some drinks out of people's hands.
6. Harriet suggests that I take some baths.
7. I have to break some bad habits this year.
8. John gained some weight after he stopped smoking.
9. I ran some errands for my wife.
10. I smoked some cigarettes after dinner.

Grammatically Complete Sentences

To be grammatically complete, an English sentence should have a subject and a verb. In the story "Diary of a Quitter," some sentences don't have a subject or don't have a subject or verb. This is because writers of stories are allowed to break the rules if this serves a purpose in their story. By using incomplete sentences, the author of this story makes the writing sound more like an informal diary.

Expand these sentences from the story to make them grammatically complete. Add a subject and, if necessary, a verb. Add other words only if needed. Use the tense indicated for verbs. There may be more than one way to expand a sentence.

EXAMPLE: This is supposed to be my edgy day, but I'm fine. Sharp. Alert. (simple present)

This is supposed to be my edgy day, but I'm fine. I'm sharp. I'm alert. *or*

This is supposed to be my edgy day, but I'm fine. I feel sharp. I feel alert.

1. Breakfast today: sliced apple, quartered orange, eight grapes, raw carrots. (simple past)
2. Another warm bath. (simple present)
3. Two warm baths today. (simple past)
4. Coffee for breakfast. (simple present)
5. Discovered something interesting.
6. No cigarettes for a week. (simple past)
7. Backed out of the garage.
8. Took a warm bath.
9. A cigarette hangover today. (simple past)

Irregular Verbs: *To Be, To Do,* and *To Have*

The most commonly used irregular verbs are *to be, to do,* and *to have*.

Exercise 1

Fill in the correct present tense form of the verb in parentheses.

EXAMPLE: a. I _____*am*_____ tired of taking baths.
(to be)

b. _____*Do*_____ you want to run errands?
(To do)

c. She _____*has*_____ a wonderful suggestion.
(to have)

1. Smoking _____ a bad habit.
(to be)

2. Harriet and I _____ happy with my decision.
(to be)

3. I _____ waiting for Aunt Garnet.
(to be)

4. Aunt Garnet _____ not know that she smells
(to do)
of smoke.

5. Mr. Peebles _____ always trying to quit.
(to be)

6. _____ eating this food make you feel like a monkey?
(To do)

7. Because we can't smoke, we _____ always hungry.
(to be)

8. Because Harriet and I gave up cigarettes, we now

_____ more money.
(to have)

9. My fingers _____ like prunes.
(to be)

(Continued on next page)

10. _____ you go to sleep early?
    (To do)

11. _____ taking baths make you feel less edgy?
    (To do)

12. _____ you have the taillight I need for my car?
    (To do)

13. My neighbor and I _____ a lot to talk about.
    (to have)

Exercise 2

Change any five (5) of the above sentences to the future tense.

Subject–Verb Agreement

Choose the correct word from those in parentheses.

EXAMPLE: Deep within me a small voice _____*keeps*_____
                                        (keep/keeps)

answering, "The heck you don't."

1. Alcohol _____ you want to smoke.
   (make/makes)

2. Kicking the cigarette habit _____ people put on
   (make/makes)
   weight.

3. My sliced apple, quartered orange, eight grapes, and raw carrot

   _____ me of something.
   (remind/reminds)

4. It's what they _____ the monkeys at the zoo.
   (give/gives)

5. Most people who _____ smoking
   (quit/quits)
   _____ irritable on the fourth day.
   (get/gets)

6. My abstinence _____ nothing to do with the things
   (have/has)
   I said today.

7. I lie in the tub and _____ how badly the bathroom
   (notice/notices)
   _____ painting.
   (need/needs)

8. I can honestly say that quitting cigarettes _____
   (are/is)
   as easy as taking candy from a baby.

9. My taste buds, deadened by years of smoking, _____
   (have/has)
   begun to flex their little muscles again.

10. Running errands _____ me want to watch TV,
    (make/makes)
    which _____ me want to smoke.
    (make/makes)
11. Warm baths _____ me want to smoke.
    (make/makes)
12. So _____ cold baths.
    (do/does)
13. So _____ going without a bath.
    (do/does)

*F*OLLOW UP

Topics for Discussion

1. In the story, the writer does certain things every day. Describe your daily routine. Use some of the following words in your description.

alarm clock	transportation
shave	telephone
dress	mail
shower	shopping
hair	news
meals	

2. Do you think that breaking the cigarette habit is just a matter of exercising willpower? Why or why not?

3. If you used to smoke, how did you quit?

4. If you never smoked, is there any habit you tried to break? If so, what happened?

5. If you are a nonsmoker, does smoking bother you? If so, how do you deal with a person who insists on smoking even though you have told him or her that you don't like it?

6. If you smoke, do you want to quit? Why or why not?

Topics for Writing

1. Did you ever try kicking a habit? How did you go about it? In three paragraphs, describe how you did it.

2. Write a paragraph to a friend who is a smoker, explaining why smoking is bad for him or her.

(Continued on next page)

3. In the library, find two articles dealing with the unhealthy effects of smoking cigarettes. Write a three-paragraph summary of the two articles.

4a. Keep a diary for a few days (or think about the past week and write a diary entry for each day). Your diary can be about something particular in your life (like the narrator's diary about trying to quit smoking) or it can be about your life in general during these days.

4b. Write a short story that, like "Diary of a Quitter," is written as a diary. Your story can be serious or humorous, and it can be about anything you want to make it about. The narrator might be trying to break a bad habit, to solve a problem, to improve a relationship—or anything else you can think of.

A Visitor in the Piano Warehouse—Part I

—WILLIAM SAROYAN

A Visitor in the Piano Warehouse—Part I

◆ **PREVIEWING THE STORY**

Look at the picture, the title, and the first paragraph of the story. Answer the questions, explaining each answer.

1. Where does the scene in the picture take place?

2. What do you think is happening in the picture? What are these people doing?

3. What do you think the story might be about?

◆ **THINKING ABOUT THE TOPIC**

Think about and answer the following questions.

1. Think of a country other than the United States. If you want to find a job in a company there, what do you do? With whom do you speak?

2. How would you prepare for a job interview?

3. If all that you knew about a job was that many people had quit it, would you be willing to take this job? Would you be willing to take the job if you would get a pay raise each month?

I work in the warehouse[1] of Sligo, Baylie on Bryant Street between First and Second, directly under the curve of the Fremont Street ramp[2] of the Bay Bridge in San Francisco. The warehouse is one block long, and half a block wide. It is full of pianos.

Sligo, Baylie is an old San Francisco music store located at the corner of Grant Avenue and Geary Street, about two miles from the warehouse. It has been in business one hundred and eleven years. The company occupies its own building of six floors. It deals in everything pertaining to* music, as well as in radios, televisions, refrigerators, deep-freeze boxes, stoves, sporting goods, and many other things. I have never met Lucander Sligo III, who owns and operates the business.

The first Lucander Sligo founded the company with Elton Baylie. The business was a piano business exclusively[3] for quite a number of years. Baylie had no sons, but his daughter Eltonia went into the company. Baylie hoped she would marry the first Lucander's son, but Eltonia married a man named Spezzafly when she was forty-four and he was ten or eleven years younger. Eltonia's husband wasn't interested in pianos, if in fact he was interested in Eltonia. He certainly wasn't interested in their son. He left Eltonia before the boy was born.

The staff[4] at the warehouse of Sligo, Baylie consists of Eltonia's son, Oliver Morgan Spezzafly, now sixty-nine, and myself, Ashland Clewpor, twenty-four.

I have been at the warehouse a year and a half.

I applied for work at the personnel department[5] of Sligo, Baylie, on the sixth floor. The girl in charge was quite impressed with the facts of my background,[6] but she regretted very much that there was no opening.[7]

"Unless," she said, "you wouldn't mind* working at the warehouse."

"What kind of work is it?"

She then told me about O. M. Spezzafly. She warned[8] me that over the past twenty-five years nobody had worked for him for longer than a month.

"Why not?"

She tried to tell me as nicely as possible that O. M., as she called him, was certainly entitled to* an important position with the firm, with an important yearly salary,[9] but that it had been absolutely[10] necessary

[1] building for storing things

[2] slanted roadway

[3] only

[4] group of workers

[5] people who deal with workers

[6] personal history

[7] available job

[8] told of a danger

[9] pay

[10] entirely

35

twenty-five years ago to make him manager[11] of the warehouse—or, to put it bluntly,* to get him out of the way.*

As manager of the warehouse, O. M. had asked for a staff, she said, and Lucander Sligo III had insisted on* letting O. M. have a secretary, a bookkeeper, a janitor, and an all-around piano man, one who could tune[12] and repair pianos. The secretary quit[13] after a week, though, and the others within a month. Little by little O. M. became adjusted to* the idea of having a staff of only one.

[12] adjust a musical instrument

[13] left

"What does the job pay?" I said.

"Sixty-five dollars a week to start. There is a five-dollar raise[14] every month, however."

[14] increase

"For how long?"

"For as long as you keep the job."

"Suppose I keep it three years?"

"You will get a raise of five dollars every month."

"What are my duties?"[15]

[15] responsibilities

"O. M. will let you know."

"Can you give me an idea of what they *might* be?"

"I'm afraid not," the girl said. "All I know is that you will be at the warehouse eight hours a day Monday through Friday. I'm afraid I can't urge[16] you to take the job."

[16] strongly advise

Half an hour later I was at the warehouse, knocking at the front door. I knocked because the door was locked. At last I heard footsteps, light and swift, and the door was swung open. I saw a tall man who wore a dark business suit. I introduced myself, and he asked me to come to his office, the door of which was only a few feet from the entrance to the warehouse.

Mr. Spezzafly's office was large and handsomely[17] furnished. His desk was enormous[18] and expensive. His chair was made of black leather. Behind his chair was a large portrait in oils of his grandfather Elton Baylie, and beside it a portrait of his mother Eltonia.

[17] nicely; beautifully

[18] very large

The interview[19] was short, although Mr. Spezzafly examined the form I had filled out at the personnel department.

[19] meeting between employer and applicant

"Ashland Clewpor?"

"Yes, sir."

"Let me show you your office, Mr. Clewpor."

We walked through pianos of all kinds, but not through a path of any kind, to the far end of the warehouse where a fence had been put around a small area. The fence began two feet from the floor and stopped at five feet. We entered through swinging doors and I saw a small area entirely bare of anything except a plain flat-top desk and a plain unvarnished[20] chair. There was a telephone on the desk. Nothing else.

[20] not shiny

"Sit down, please, Mr. Clewpor."

I sat at the desk.

"Very good," Mr. Spezzafly said, and left.

I sat at the desk without moving for about ten minutes, and then I drew open the drawers of the desk and found all six of them empty. The whole office was a desk and a chair, surrounded by a fence.

At a quarter of five I decided to use the telephone, more for something to do than somebody to talk to. I thought I would call Newbegin's and ask if they could recommend a good book on pianos. I began to dial Information for the number, but while I was doing so I heard somebody say, "Yes?"

It was Mr. Spezzafly.

"I thought I would telephone Newbegin's to see if they have a good history of the piano."

"O. M. Spezzafly speaking."

"Yes, sir."

"May I ask who's calling?"

"There must be something the matter with the phone, Mr. Spezzafly," I said. "This is Ashland Clewpor."

"What is it, Mr. Clewpor?"

"I was wondering if I might telephone Newbegin's."

"What is Newbegin's?"

"It's a bookstore, sir."

"I'll call you back," Mr. Spezzafly said.

I thought he meant in a few minutes.

He called me back on Friday at five minutes to five.

"Mr. Clewpor," he said, "on your way out please stop at my desk and pick up your check."

"Yes, sir."

The check was in a green plate that might have served as an ash tray.

"You'll find it there every Friday," Mr. Spezzafly said.

"Yes, sir. Thank you."

I took the check and folded it, so that if there was anything he might wish to tell me there would be time for him to do so.

"Well done," he said. "That was a perfect fold."

I waited a moment in the hope that he would say something about what I might expect next week, but he said nothing.

Saturday morning I visited the personnel department of Sligo, Baylie, and the girl there said, "Well?"

"I was wondering if there is anything you might care to tell me about Mr. Spezzafly."

"You haven't come to quit?"

"No, I don't think I have."

"What did you do all week?"

"Nothing."

"What did he do?"

"I don't know."

"Do you think him odd?"[21]

"He doesn't *look* odd."

"You plan to stay, then?"

"Is there an opening here?"

"Well," the girl said, "to be perfectly honest, there *is,* but it's in the stove department, and it's sixty-five a week, with no raises at all. Certainly not for a year or two. Would you like to meet the manager of the stove department?"

"Well, if I kept my job with Mr. Spezzafly for a year I'd be getting a salary of one hundred and twenty five dollars a week, wouldn't I?"

"Yes, that's right," the girl said.

"That's pretty good, isn't it?"

"Yes, it is."

"Well, I'm not married."

"Yes, I noticed that you're not when I read your application[22] last Monday."

"Well, after a year with Mr. Spezzafly if I said to you will you be my wife, what would you say?"

"I'm married," the girl said. "Do you want to meet the manager of the stove department?"

"No," I said. "Is there anything you can tell me about Mr. Spezzafly? I mean, what are my duties?"

[21] unusual, crazy

[22] form filled out when requesting a job

"Well," the girl said, "if you've decided to stay with Mr. Spezzafly another week, why not ask him Monday morning?"

Mr. Spezzafly was standing outside the door of his office at eight o'clock Monday morning.

"I appreciate punctuality,"[23] he said. "The time is one minute to eight. I am apt to* be here at *ten* minutes to eight, but it is quite all right for you to be here at one minute to eight."

"Yes, sir."

"I also appreciate a good appearance.[24] A man who comes to work Monday morning looking fit[25] is a man who is going to look fit all week."

"Mr. Spezzafly, what are my duties?"

"My boy," Mr. Spezzafly said, "your work is waiting for you in your office."

He nodded courteously[26] and went into his office. I walked through the pianos and went into my office. I expected to see a stack of papers on my desk, but there wasn't anything there. I sat down and tried to guess who she had married, but I couldn't. A girl who is married is married, that's all.

The second week went by exactly like the first. Friday afternoon at five I picked up my check and went home. Saturday morning I went back to the personnel department, because I had to see her again.

"There's an opening in the refrigerator department," she said. "Would you like to meet the manager of the refrigerator department?"

"Who is he?"

"Mr. Stavros."

"How much is the salary?"

"Sixty-five, but there's no promise of a raise. Aren't you happy at the warehouse?"

"I don't know what I'm supposed to do."

"Yes, that's how it goes."*

"I made a path through the pianos."

"Did Mr. Spezzafly approve?"[27]

"He didn't say."

"Did he *use* the path?"

"No, but the day I made the path he phoned at a quarter to five and said that whenever I answer the phone in the future I should say, 'Ashland speaking'. I *had* been saying 'Hello'."

[23] quality of being on time

[24] the way a person looks

[25] right; suitable

[26] politely

[27] say or think it is good

"I believe he likes the path you made."

"Do you mean I should go ahead and do things like that?"

"Yes, I think so."

"Shouldn't I try to *sell* a piano?"

"Has anybody asked for one?"

"No, but he keeps the front door locked."

"Well, it *is* a warehouse, not a salesroom."

"What are the pianos for?"

"People trade in* old pianos for various modern things, and we put the old pianos in the warehouse, that's all."

"Do you ever take them out?"

"There isn't much demand for old pianos."

"We've got a hundred and twenty-three of them. I counted them."

"Do you like being among a lot of pianos?"

"Yes, I *do.* I like to see those pianos every morning. Of course, I see them all day, too, but I mean when I go in there every morning I *especially* enjoy seeing them. There they are, I mean. All of them. All kinds of them. Who did you marry?"

[28] a large California bank

"My husband is an accountant at Wells, Fargo.[28] The refrigerator department is full of laughter and jokes all day long, because Mr. Stavros is such a humorous man. Would you like to meet him?"

"No, but if you have a sister, I'd like to meet her."

[29] nice-looking

"I don't have a sister. There are three rather attractive[29] girls in the refrigerator department, though. Perhaps you ought to leave the warehouse."

[30] aim in life

"I never *expected* to work in a warehouse. My ambition[30] has always been to be famous."

[31] wrote quickly

"A lot of people think Mr. Stavros would have been famous if he had gone on the stage." She scribbled[31] something on a piece of paper with some mimeographed typing on it. She folded the piece of paper and held it out to me.

"What is it?"

"An introduction to Mr. Stavros."

"I don't think I want to leave the warehouse just yet." ◆

Idioms and Phrases*

pertaining to	*connected to*
would (not) mind	*would (not) dislike*
was entitled to	*had the right to*
to put it bluntly	*to say something plainly, without trying to be polite*
get (someone) out of the way	*to put (someone) in a place where (he or she) can't cause difficulties*
insisted on	*made a strong demand*
became adjusted to	*got used to*
apt to	*likely to*
That's how it goes.	*That's what happens.*
trade in	*exchange*

POST-READING

Comprehension

1. In what city was Sligo, Baylie located? What did it sell?

2. Who was Mr. Spezzafly? Why was he put in charge of the warehouse?

3. What did the woman in the personnel department tell Ashland about the job in the warehouse? What couldn't she tell him about it? What did Ashland decide?

4. What would Ashland's weekly salary be by the end of the year?

5. Describe Mr. Spezzafly's office and Ashland's office.

6. What did Ashland do during his first week of work?

7. What kind of pianos were in the warehouse?

8. Why did Ashland go back to the personnel department? What happened when he went back?

9. What did Ashland say his ambition was?

Responding to the Story

1. Why do you think Mr. Spezzafly had to be gotten out of the way?

2. Do you think Mr. Spezzafly liked being in the warehouse, or do you think he minded it? Explain your answer.

3. Why do you think no one was able to work for Mr. Spezzafly for more than a month?

(Continued on next page)

4. Why do you think Ashland accepted the job at the piano warehouse?

5. Why did Ashland continue to work for Mr. Spezzafly even though there were other openings in the company?

6. What made Mr. Spezzafly an unusual boss? How would you feel about working for him?

7. The story continues in the next chapter. Will Mr. Spezzafly become very different, or will he remain the same? Will Ashland stay in the warehouse, or will he move to another job? What do you think?

Vocabulary Builder

Show that you know the definition of the underlined word by circling a, b, *or* c.

1. I work in the warehouse.
   a. office building
   b. building with salesrooms
   c. building for storing things

2. This business was a piano business exclusively.
   a. mainly
   b. only
   c. in the past

3. A personnel department is the section of a company which deals with
   a. customers
   b. sales
   c. workers

4. A raise means
   a. an increase in salary
   b. a decrease in salary
   c. a move to another department

5. That Mr. Spezzafly's <u>interview</u> with Ashland was short implies that
   a. he didn't ask Ashland many questions
   b. he didn't give Ashland many responsibilities
   c. he didn't offer Ashland a raise

6. Do you think him <u>odd</u>?
   a. intelligent
   b. handsome
   c. unusual

7. I appreciate his <u>punctuality</u>.
   a. the quality of being polite
   b. the quality of being on time
   c. the quality of being clean and neat

8. Ashland had a definite <u>ambition</u>.
   a. way of talking
   b. schedule for work
   c. aim in life

9. It was <u>absolutely</u> necessary to get him out of the way.
   a. increasingly
   b. entirely
   c. possibly

10. <u>Enormous</u> is an antonym of (means the opposite of)
    a. ugly
    b. unknown
    c. small

11. <u>Courteously</u> is an antonym of
    a. rudely
    b. softly
    c. slowly

12. <u>Attractive</u> is an antonym of
    a. busy
    b. lovely
    c. ugly

Idiom Exercise

Show that you know the definition of the underlined word by circling a, b, *or* c.

1. The phrase <u>pertaining to</u> music means
   a. playing with
   b. connected to
   c. dancing to

2. I <u>wouldn't mind</u> working at the warehouse.
   a. would love
   b. would not like
   c. would not dislike

3. I am <u>apt to</u> be here at ten minutes to eight.
   a. likely to
   b. willing to
   c. able to

4. I want to <u>trade in</u> my violin for a piano.
   a. play
   b. bring
   c. exchange

Word Forms

Fill in the correct word form from those listed. Each form should be used.

1. apply, applying, application
   a. When you're _____ for a job, be sure to send a resume.
   b. You must _____ for this job in person.
   c. Your job _____ should be neat.

2. appear, appearance, appearing, appeared
   a. Your _____ is important when you apply for a job.
   b. _____ for the interview on time is also important.
   c. Will you _____ in person to pick up your paycheck?
   d. When I saw him last time, he _____ nervous.

Want Ads

Study carefully the two want ads below. Based on the ads and your knowledge of job-search vocabulary, answer the questions that follow.

Job A

> **SALES/RETAIL**
> Experienced furniture salesperson needed for growing company.
> Hours flexible. Excellent opportunity.
> **815-682-4446 or 4447**

Job B

> **SALES OPPORTUNITY**
> National Rental Car Corp. seeks personable, professional indiv for its sales representative program.
> Exp in sales, automotive or insurance industry helpful. Exc oppty for a dedicated indiv to join an industry leader. Salary, bonus, company car & bnfts. Immd opening in Manhattan area. Send resume & salary hist to: Rental Car Corp., Regional Offices, 1603 Franklin Dr., Elmville, NY 73072
> Attn: Ms. Maffucci

1. What other information would you need to know about Job A in order to help you decide if you are interested in the job?

2. What should you do if you are interested in Job A?

3. What should you do if you are interested in Job B?

4. What is a resume, and what information does it usually include? What is usually sent with a resume?

5. If you had no sales experience, could you apply for Job A? If you had no sales experience, could you apply for Job B?

6. If you don't drive a car, would you apply for Job B?

7. Which job do you think would offer more money? Why?

8. Which position offers extras? What are they?

9. What is a bonus? What are benefits that companies might offer?

10. Which job seems to offer more opportunity for promotion?

Job Applications

When you apply for a job, you are usually asked to fill out a job application. It is important to fill it out accurately and completely.

Look at the sample application below and answer the questions on page 48.

Application For Employment

This is an Equal Opportunity Employer	PLEASE COMPLETE **ALL** SECTIONS, EVEN IF YOU ARE ATTACHING A RESUME

NAME: LAST   FIRST   MIDDLE   HOME PHONE NO.

ADDRESS   WORK PHONE NO.

CITY   STATE   ZIP CODE   SOCIAL SECURITY NO.

POSITION DESIRED   SALARY REQUIREMENT   HOW WERE YOU REFERRED TO US? (CHECK ONE)
☐ Ad   ☐ Agency
☐ Walk-In   ☐ Friend/Referral
☐ School/College   ☐ Other

HAVE YOU EVER BEEN EMPLOYED BY US?
☐ YES   ☐ NO   IF YES, WHERE?

GENERAL INFORMATION

ARE ANY OF YOUR RELATIVES EMPLOYED BY US?
☐ YES   ☐ NO   LOCATION

RELATIONSHIP(S)

HAVE YOU BEEN CONVICTED OF ANY FELONY CRIME IN THE LAST SEVEN YEARS? (A CONVICTION MAY NOT NECESSARILY BE A BAR TO EMPLOYMENT)
☐ YES   ☐ NO   IF YES, EXPLAIN:

NAME UNDER WHICH YOU ARE KNOWN TO REFERENCES. (IF DIFFERENT FROM THAT LISTED ABOVE)

ARE YOU UNDER 16 YEARS OF AGE? ☐ YES   ☐ NO
(COMPANY POLICY PROHIBITS THE HIRING OF THOSE INDIVIDUALS **UNDER** 16 YEARS OF AGE)

DO YOU DESIRE:
☐ FULL-TIME   ☐ PART-TIME   ☐ TEMPORARY

PLEASE INDICATE THE HOURS THAT YOU ARE AVAILABLE TO WORK ON EACH OF THESE DAYS:

	SUNDAY	MONDAY	TUESDAY	WEDNESDAY	THURSDAY	FRIDAY	SATURDAY
FROM (Hours)							
TO (Hours)							

Should your availability change during the course of your employment, it may impact your employment status based upon our business needs. While we may be able to accommodate your availability limitations upon hire, we do not guarantee that we will be able to support these limitations in the future. Should our business needs change, we may require an adjustment in your availability.

EDUCATION

SCHOOL NAME	ADDRESS	FROM	TO	DEGREE/DIPLOMA
HIGH SCHOOL				DIPLOMA ☐YES ☐NO TYPE:
BUSINESS/VOCATION SCHOOL				DIPLOMA ☐YES ☐NO TYPE:
COMMUNITY COLLEGE/UNIVERSITY				DIPLOMA ☐YES ☐NO TYPE:
COMMUNITY COLLEGE/UNIVERSITY				DIPLOMA ☐YES ☐NO TYPE:

WORK EXPERIENCE	**Application For Employment**

COMPANY	PHONE NUMBER

ADDRESS STREET CITY STATE ZIP	EMPLOYMENT DATES FROM: TO:

POSITION HELD	STARTING SALARY	PRESENT/FINAL SALARY

IMMEDIATE SUPERVISOR	TITLE	MAY WE CONTACT YOUR PRESENT EMPLOYER? IF NOT, WHEN? ☐ YES ☐ NO

REASON FOR LEAVING	

COMPANY	PHONE NUMBER

ADDRESS STREET CITY STATE ZIP	EMPLOYMENT DATES FROM: TO:

POSITION HELD	STARTING SALARY	FINAL SALARY

IMMEDIATE SUPERVISOR	TITLE	ADDITIONAL REFERENCE

REASON FOR LEAVING	PHONE NUMBER

COMPANY	PHONE NUMBER

ADDRESS STREET CITY STATE ZIP	EMPLOYMENT DATES FROM: TO:

POSITION HELD	STARTING SALARY	FINAL SALARY

IMMEDIATE SUPERVISOR	TITLE	ADDITIONAL REFERENCE

REASON FOR LEAVING	PHONE NUMBER

HAVE YOU EVER BEEN DISCHARGED OR FORCED TO RESIGN ANY POSITION? ☐ YES ☐ NO   IF YES, EXPLAIN IN DETAIL.

LIST THREE PERSONAL OR ADDITIONAL PROFESSIONAL REFERENCES (NON-FAMILY MEMBERS):	NAME	PHONE NUMBER	PRESENT EMPLOYER	RELATIONSHIP

ADDITIONAL COMMENTS - PLEASE FEEL FREE TO WRITE ANY ADDITIONAL COMMENTS WHICH MIGHT ASSIST US IN PLACING YOU (INCLUDING PROFESSIONAL ORGANIZATIONS, CAREER-RELATED ACTIVITIES, SKILLS OR QUALIFICATIONS) WITHIN OUR ORGANIZATION.

PLEASE READ CAREFULLY:

All of our employees may be bonded, and a thorough investigation will be made. It is vitally important that all questions be answered accurately as requested. I understand and agree that if hired, my employment may be terminated at any time if I inaccurately provided or omitted information upon completion of this form or when such facts are discovered by my employer.

I hereby certify that my answers to the questions on this application are true and correct to the best of my knowledge. I give you, the employer, or the applicable subsidiary, the right to verify all requested information and to otherwise investigate my qualifications for employment which may include, but not be limited to, securing additional information. I understand that a bonding and security investigation may be made whereby information is obtained through personal interviews with third parties, such as family members, business associates, financial sources, friends, neighbors, or others with whom I am acquainted. I hereby release all persons from any liability in this investigation.

I understand that any offer of employment is conditioned upon the satisfactory completion of this verification process and that the company will hire only those individuals who are legally authorized to work in the United States and who present acceptable proof of their lawful employment status and identity.

APPLICANT'S SIGNATURE _____   DATE _____

HUMAN RESOURCES DEPARTMENT USE ONLY					
STARTING DATE	SALARY	PAY GRADE	☐ EXEMPT ☐ NON-EXEMPT	DATE JOB OFFERED	DEPARTMENT/STORE NO.
EMPLOYEE NO.	POSITION			HIRED BY	

7003 6/94

1. Under "Work Experience," what is meant by:
   a. company
   b. position held
   c. immediate supervisor
   d. reasons for leaving

2. What are references?

3. Using your dictionary, explain the following terms:
   a. salary
   b. convicted
   c. felony
   d. available

Now pretend that you are applying for a job. Complete the application.

STRUCTURE

Some Confusing Subjects

It is usually easy to tell when a subject is plural because it has *-s* or *-es* added to it.

EXAMPLE: pianos (more than one piano)
 buses (more than one bus)

There are several words that stand for a group of people or things. These words are called collective nouns. Here are some of them:

army	orchestra	information	faculty
class	family	public	company
crowd	group	staff	personnel
committee	team	news	

Collective nouns usually are singular because they represent a single group.

EXAMPLE: The crowd is waiting for a warehouse sale.
 (The entire crowd is waiting together.)

Sometimes, though, collective nouns are plural. They are plural when the group that they represent is not acting together.

EXAMPLE: The crowd are arguing among themselves about whether the pianos are in good condition.

In this example, the crowd is not acting as a single unit. Members of the crowd are disagreeing with each other.

Fill in the correct form of the verb in the following sentences. Make sure that the subject and verb agree.

1. The class (is, are) learning how to fill out job applications.
2. The class (is, are) arguing among themselves about whether there should be a question about age on the application.
3. The news in the office (is, are) not always good.
4. The committee (meet, meets) every Wednesday to discuss new personnel.
5. My family (consist, consists) of a father, a mother, a sister, and a brother.
6. Politics (does, do) not fascinate Ashland Clewpor.
7. The personnel at Sligo, Baylie (is, are) very difficult.
8. Athletics (interest, interests) Mr. Spezzafly very little.
9. The staff (disagree, disagrees) with each other about salary raises.
10. The United States (is, are) trying to sell more pianos to Japan.

Defining Job Duties

Look at the pictures of people at work. Choose three of the pictures and list the job duties for each position illustrated in the picture.

Word Order: Questions

Arrange the following groups of words in customary order to make complete questions.

like
manager
meet
to   EXAMPLE: Would you like to meet the manager?
the
would
you

1. duties
   my
   what
   are

2. how
   is
   much
   salary
   the

3. kind
   is
   it
   what
   work
   of

4. here
   there
   an
   opening
   is

5. odd
   think
   you
   him
   do

6. ask
   I
   calling
   may
   who's

7. a
   I
   to
   piano
   sell
   try
   shouldn't

Forming Questions

Exercise 1

Form questions from the words given. Use the present tense. Add do *if it is needed; do not add any other words.*

EXAMPLE: What/BE/my duties?
What are my duties?

1. Would/you/LIKE/to meet him
2. What/the job/PAY
3. Can/you/GIVE/me an idea
4. What/you/DO/all week
5. You/WANT/to meet the manager
6. You/TAKE/the pianos out
7. Whom/BE/you married to

Exercise 2

Write a question for each of the following answers. (As above, some questions are yes/no *questions and some are* wh- *questions.)*

EXAMPLE: Yes, there is an opening here.
Is there an opening here?

1. Newbegin's is a bookstore.
2. Yes, Newbegin's is in San Francisco.
3. Yes, I like being among the pianos.
4. No, I can't tell you what your duties are.
5. The salary is sixty-five dollars.
6. My ambition is to be famous.

Exercise 3

ROLE PLAY: Work with a partner. You are the manager of a personnel department of a store. Your partner is coming to apply for a sales job (or an office job). You will interview him or her. Write a list of questions to ask (if you want, refer to the application on pages 46–47 to get some ideas about questions to ask). Ask these questions and, based on your partner's answers, decide whether to give him or her the job. Then switch roles: Your partner writes the questions and interviews you.

Present Perfect Tense

The present perfect tense is used for an action that began in the past and continues in the present. It is formed by the present tense of the verb *to have* and the past participle of the verb. When we use the present perfect tense, we do not say precisely when the action took place.

EXAMPLE: Since I came to the piano warehouse, I _____*have learned*_____
                     a great deal about Mr. Spezzafly.   (learn)

Complete the following sentences by adding the present perfect form of the verb in parentheses.

1. I _____ for this man for twenty years.
   (work)

2. He _____ this piano more than once.
   (tune)

3. The personnel director _____ him many times to
   (urge)
   take a job in other departments.

4. I _____ a note to my boss to tell him that I am
   (scribble)
   taking two hours for lunch.

5. _____ you _____ for a job in
                          (look)
   the classified section of the newspaper?

6. I _____ to take the job.
   (decide)

7. _____ you _____ your
                          (locate)
   manager's telephone number?

8. Ashland _____ his blue suit to every job
   (wear)
   interview.

9. The personnel director _____ me about the
   (tell)
   importance of being on time.

10. I _____ every appointment I have ever
    (keep)
    _____ .
    (make)

11. I _____ many famous people in my life.
    (know)

12. Ashland _____ already _____
                                                      (get)
    two pay raises.

13. Mr. Spezzafly _____ the door locked for the
    (keep)
    past twenty years.

14. _____ they _____ your salary
    (raise)
    yet?

15. _____ you _____ a raise yet?
    (get)

Past Tense

Many verbs add *-ed* to form the past tense. For example, the past tense
form of *walk* is *walked,* and the past tense form of *hurry* is *hurried*
(notice that the *y* changes to *i*). Other verbs have irregular past tense
forms, which must be learned.

Fill in each blank with the past tense form of the verb indicated.
(Some forms are regular; others are irregular.)

EXAMPLE: Baylie _____*hoped*_____ she would marry Lucander's
          (hope)
          son.

1. The business _____ a piano business exclusively
   (be)
   for quite a number of years.

2. Baylie _____ no sons, but his daughter Eltonia
   (have)
   _____ into the business.
   (go)

3. Eltonia _____ a man named Spezzafly.
   (marry)

4. He _____ Eltonia before their son
   (leave)
   _____ born.
   (be)

5. I _____ for work at the personnel department of
   (apply)
   Sligo, Baylie.

6. She then _____ me about O. M. Spezzafly.
   (tell)

7. The secretary _____ after a week.
   (quit)

8. O. M. _____ adjusted to the idea of having a
   (become)
   staff of only one.

(Continued on next page)

9. "What does the job pay?" I _____.
                                 (ask)

10. I _____ myself, and he _____
       (introduce)   (ask)
    me to come to his office.

11. Mr. Spezzafly _____ the form from the
                       (examine)
    personnel department.

12. We _____ through pianos of all kinds.
           (walk)

13. We _____ through the swinging doors and I
           (enter)
    _____ a small area.
       (see)

14. I _____ at the desk.
      (sit)

15. I _____ all six of the desk drawers empty.
      (find)

16. I _____ to use the telephone.
      (decide)

17. I _____ I would call Newbegin's.
      (think)

18. He _____ me back several days later.
      (call)

19. I _____ a path through the pianos.
      (make)

20. She _____ the piece of paper and
       (fold)
    _____ it out to me.
      (hold)

A Visitor in the Piano Warehouse—Part II

—WILLIAM SAROYAN

Monday morning at one minute to eight Mr. Spezzafly was standing outside the door of his office.

"Ash," he said, "if you go straight to your office and sit at your desk, I'm going to try something."

I went to my office and sat at my desk, and after two or three minutes the telephone buzzed and I lifted the receiver.

"Ashland speaking," I said.

"Ash," Mr. Spezzafly said, "I'm thinking of leaving the front door unlatched,[1] so that it can be opened from the street without a key. I thought I'd try that this morning, and possibly this afternoon."

"Yes, sir."

"If somebody comes in, I'll let you know by telephone."

"Yes, sir."

"In case I don't happen to notice, though, and you do—"

Mr. Spezzafly stopped. I waited a moment, and then I said, "Yes, sir?"

"Well, Ash, what I mean is, find out who it is."

"Yes, sir. Shall I let you know?"

"I don't think so, Ash. This is only an experiment."

"Yes, sir."

Nobody came in all day Monday. Tuesday morning at half past ten my telephone buzzed and Mr. Spezzafly said, "I just want you to know, Ash, that I've left the door unlatched again."

"Yes, sir."

"On second thought,* if someone comes in, give me a ring. Just say, 'Visitor in the warehouse'. I'll understand."

"Yes, sir. Visitor in the warehouse."

"Precisely."

Nobody came in, but at a quarter of five I thought I'd phone him to ask if he wanted me to try to sell a piano.

When he lifted the receiver he said, "Visitor in the warehouse, Ash?"

"No, sir."

"Dang."[2]

"I called to ask if you'd like me to try to sell a piano."

"Ash," Mr. Spezzafly said, "let's just call when there's a visitor in the warehouse."

56

"Yes, sir."

There wasn't a visitor all week. Friday afternoon I picked up my check and went home, and Saturday morning I went up to the personnel department again, and the girl there said, "I've got a rather exciting position to offer you in the sporting goods department. Mr. Plattock wants a likely-looking man to demonstrate[3] the rowing machine[4] and the limbering-up bicycle.[4] Would you like to meet Mr. Plattock?"

[3] show how something works
[4] exercise machines

"I don't know."

"You will be permitted to wear sports clothing supplied by Sligo, Baylie, and I have an idea you will make an excellent impression."*

She began to scribble on the small piece of paper again, but I just wasn't thinking about demonstrating a rowing machine or a limbering-up bicycle, I was thinking about having a visitor in the warehouse.

"Could you come to the warehouse next Monday during your lunch hour?"

"I *could*—of course," the girl said. "Is there a particular reason why I *should*, however?"

"Well, Mr. Spezzafly is trying out something new. He's leaving the front door unlatched, so that anybody who wants to come into the warehouse from Bryant Street can do so, but all last week nobody came in. I thought if you were to come in, I could telephone Mr. Spezzafly."

"I see."

"Afterwards, we could go to lunch at the place next to the S.P. depot."

"I generally have lunch with my husband at a little place next door to Wells, Fargo."

"Could you skip[5] lunch with your husband on Monday?"

[5] not do; not go to

"You'd rather not meet Mr. Plattock, then?"

"I don't think so. You see, when I start something, I like to try to see it through."

"Oh? You feel you've started something, do you?"

"Yes, I do."

"What is it that you feel you've started?"

"I've started to understand Mr. Spezzafly."

"Really?"

"Yes, and a few other things, too."

"What else have you started to understand?"

[6] very well known,
very good

"Well, being famous[6], for instance.* Now, being famous the way famous people are famous is not *really* being famous, but being famous the way Mr. Spezzafly's famous, that's really being famous. And a few others I know."

"Everybody at Sligo, Baylie has known about Mr. Spezzafly's fame for years. Who are the others?"

"Well, the way *you're* famous seems to me to be a way that's more famous than the famous movie actresses are famous."

"Well, that's very nice of you, but hardly anybody in the whole world knows me."

"That's the part I'm beginning to understand. You're famous without very many people knowing you, but the ones who *do* know you, *they* know you're famous."

"How do you know they do?"

"Well, I hardly know you, and I know you're famous, so just imagine how it is with those who really know you, like your husband, or your children, if you've got any."

"I haven't got any."

"But if you had some, wouldn't they know how famous you are, though?"

"Yes, I suppose they would, at that."

"Will you visit the warehouse?"

"Well, perhaps not Monday, but perhaps Tuesday or Wednesday."

"You'll find the door unlatched. My office is in the back, on the right."

Monday I took my lunch and ate it under the Fremont Street ramp of the Bay Bridge, while Mr. Spezzafly ate his at his desk. I don't know why he eats his sandwiches in his office. I eat mine in the streets because I enjoy walking during my lunch hour.

I walk down First Street to Pier 38 or down Bryant Street to Pier 28 and I look at the ships down there, and think.

I think about the past, the present, and the future, but mainly about the future, although I can't forget the past, especially where I spent so many years in the homes of people who wanted to find out if they wanted to adopt me, and decided they didn't—about when I was fifteen, and ran away because I wanted to live my own life, and when I was eighteen and got in the Marines[7] and went to Korea and got wounded[8]

[7] branch of the military
service

[8] hurt

but didn't get killed, the way three of my pals[9] did, just spent a year in different hospitals and got discharged[10] in San Francisco when I was twenty-two.

Mostly, though, on the lunch-hour walks I think about the future.

At twelve o'clock on Tuesday I didn't leave my office, even though I had no lunch to eat. I just sat at my desk, listening. There wasn't anything to listen to, but there *might* be pretty soon, and I wanted to be ready for it. At a quarter after twelve I heard it.

It was a visitor in the warehouse.

The footsteps came closer, and then the swinging doors of my office opened.

I got on the phone.

"Visitor in the warehouse, Mr. Spezzafly."

"Who is it, Ash?"

"Girl here in a blue dress."

"Thank you, Ash."

Mr. Spezzafly hung up, I hung up, and the girl in the blue dress stepped up to my desk and held out a piece of folded paper to me. It was the introduction form of the personnel department of Sligo, Baylie, and it said: *Introducing Miss Stella Mayhew to Mr. Ashland Clewpor. P.S. Good luck.*

I walked around the desk and put my hand out, and Stella Mayhew and I shook hands.

"I'm happy to make your acquaintance,"* I said.

Stella seemed awful scared, but I was awful scared myself, because in the first place* I had expected the visitor to be the girl in the personnel department, a married girl, and in the second place* Stella was the first visitor in the warehouse, and in the third place* I had never seen a girl I liked so much.

Stella opened her handbag quickly and brought out a folded application. I unfolded it and started reading the answers she had given to the questions.

I wanted to be as businesslike as possible, so after I read a few answers I said, "I see." I read a few more answers and again I said, "I see."

And then—well, I just took her in my arms and kissed her, I knew I ought to try to be a little more businesslike, but I kept thinking about the past and the future. I kept seeing the past all smoothed out on

[9] (colloq.) friends

[10] allowed or asked to leave

account of her, and I kept seeing the future just the way I'd always wanted to see it—a little house of our own, both of us famous, and a famous son, and a little later on a famous daughter.

I was kissing Stella when the telephone buzzed.

"Ashland speaking."

"What's the visitor want, Ash?"

"I don't know, sir."

"Everything in order?"*

"Yes, sir."

"All right, Ash. I'll have my lunch, then."

"Yes, sir."

Again Mr. Spezzafly hung up and I hung up.

I took my chair around the desk and asked Stella Mayhew to please sit down, because I wanted to talk to her. She sat down and I told her about my whole life, past, present, and future, and then I said, "I mean, I'm not really a business executive or anything like that. I don't have a job to offer, but I've got a job myself, and I plan to keep it, especially if there's something nice and sensible I can do with the money I earn. I'd like to make a down payment* on a new house somewhere, but I wouldn't care to do that unless I had somebody to move in there with, to be my wife. That's the only job I can offer you—if it's all right. I've read the application and I like everything in it. And of course, I can see you. I mean, I'm glad you've been in San Francisco only a week, and I'm glad you don't have any people,[11] either, because I don't, either, and people who don't have any people—well, when they have one another, I guess it means something. Is it all right?"

"Yes, sir," Stella Mayhew said.

I was kissing her again when I heard Mr. Spezzafly coming down the path I had made through the pianos, but I just couldn't stop. Mr. Spezzafly pushed the swinging doors open, and I said, "Mr. Spezzafly, may I present[12] Miss Stella Mayhew?"

"How do you do, Miss Mayhew," Mr. Spezzafly said.

"Miss Mayhew," I said, "is the future Mrs. Ashland Clewpor."

"Well, Ash," Mr. Spezzafly said, "I think that's very nice. You couldn't have found a nicer girl if you had looked all over the world." He smiled at Stella. "And you couldn't find a nicer boy," he said.

"Thank you, sir," Stella said.

[11] relatives; family

[12] introduce

"Not at all,"* Mr. Spezzafly said. He left the office, and Stella and I listened to him walking up the path back to his office.

Then Stella told me everything she knew about her own life, past, present, and future. She tried not to cry a couple of times, and made it, too, but one time she didn't. I didn't, either.

The year and a half that I've been employed in the warehouse of Sligo, Baylie has been the happiest time of my whole life. I don't ever expect to quit, although I've asked the girl in the personnel department to stop giving me the five-dollar raise every month.

"Not yet," she says. "Plenty of time to stop the raises. How is Mr. Spezzafly?"

"Just famous, the same as ever."

"And how is your wife Stella?"

"Just famous, too, thank you."

"And how is your son?"

"My son is the most famous man in the world."

"I've got a rather attractive position in the television department I can offer you," the girl in the personnel department says, but she just says that for the fun of it, because she knows I don't want to leave the warehouse.

She knows that when I start something I like to see it through. ◆

IDIOMS AND PHRASES*

on second thought	*expression indicating the speaker has changed his/her idea or opinion*
make an (excellent) impression	*look (very good; just right) to people*
for instance	*for example*
make (one's) acquaintance	*get to know (someone)*
in the first (second, third, . . .) place	*first (secondly, thirdly)*
in order	*arranged, OK*
down payment	*part of the full price, paid at time of purchase, with the rest to come later*
Not at all.	*You're welcome.*

OST-READING

Comprehension

1. What was Mr. Spezzafly's experiment?
2. What were Ashland's childhood and early adulthood like?
3. When Ashland heard footsteps in the warehouse, whom did he expect?
4. What papers did Stella give to Ashland?
5. What did Ashland do after he read Stella's application?
6. What kind of job did he offer her?
7. What was Ashland's situation at the end of the story?

Responding to the Story

1. Why do you think Mr. Spezzafly conducted his experiment?
2. What do you think Ashland means when he says that Mr. Spezzafly, the girl in the personnel department, and others are "famous"?
3. Why do you think the girl in the personnel department sent Stella to the warehouse? What did she mean when she wrote *good luck* on the introduction form?
4. Is the meeting between Ashland and Stella believable (true to life)? Why or why not?
5. How does Ashland's past help him appreciate his present job? How does it influence his desires for the future?
6. What is your opinion of Ashland and of his life?

OCABULARY

Vocabulary Builder

Replace each underlined word with the proper synonym (word with the same meaning) from the list.

not locked	family	show
introduced	leave out	hurt
friend		

When Mr. Spezzafly left the door <u>unlatched</u>, a visitor came into
(1)
the warehouse. The visitor was a pretty young lady who had been sent
by Ashland Clewpor's <u>pal</u> in the personnel department. When Ashland
(2)
saw her, he fell in love with her. She <u>presented</u> herself to him and
(3)
handed him her job application. Ashland gave her an interview, but he
decided <u>to skip</u> most of the usual questions, and he didn't ask her to
(4)
<u>demonstrate</u> her abilities. Instead, he began telling her about how he
(5)
had been <u>wounded</u> when he was in the Marines. Then he kissed her
(6)
and said he would marry her. Neither Ashland nor Stella had <u>people</u>
(7)
of their own, but they had each other.

Now, do you think Mr. Spezzafly's experiment was a success?

Idiom Exercise

*Write a sentence of your own for each idiom. Your sentences can be
about the story or anything else.*

EXAMPLE: On his walks, Ashland thought about many things;
<u>for instance</u>, he thought about his time in the Marines.

**Over the years, he was offered many jobs; for instance,
he was offered a job in the sporting goods department.**

1. The woman in personnel was sure Ashland would *make a
good impression.*
   _____ make a(n) _____ impression.
2. *On second thought,* I don't think I'm going to work this summer.
   On second thought, _____.
3. *In the first place,* I have to see which job is closer to my house.
   In the first place, _____.
4. *In the second place,* I have to find out which job pays
more money.
   In the second place, _____.
5. He made sure everything was *in order* before he left the office
for the day.
   _____ in order _____.
6. He wanted to make a *down payment* on a small house.
   _____ down payment _____.

STRUCTURE

Sentence Combining

By combining sentences, writers can avoid having many short sentences. One way of combining sentences is to use coordinating conjunctions. The most common coordinating conjunctions are *and* and *but*. *And* means information is being added; *but* means information that is in some way contrasting is being added; for example:

I went to pick up my check, and then I went to the bank.

I went to pick up my check, but it wasn't there.

If the subjects of the sentences being combined are the same, as in the first example, the second subject can be omitted:

I went to pick up my check and then went to the bank.

A comma is used before the coordinating conjunction if there are two subjects.

Exercise 1

Combine each pair of sentences by using and *or* but, *depending on the meaning. If a subject can be omitted, omit it. Include a comma if it is needed.*

EXAMPLES: I went to my office.
I sat at my desk.
I went to my office and sat at my desk.

Nobody came in.
I phoned him anyway.
Nobody came in, but I phoned him anyway.

1. I picked up my check.
   I went home.
2. Saturday I went to the personnel department.
   The girl there said, "I've got an exciting position to offer you."
3. She offered me the sporting goods job.
   I wasn't interested in it.
4. Anyone can come into the warehouse now.
   No one comes.

5. It's nice of you to say I'm famous.

   Hardly anybody knows me.

6. I took my lunch.

   I ate it under the ramp of the bridge.

7. I didn't get killed in Korea.

   I did get wounded.

8. No one is here.

   Someone might arrive soon.

9. I walked around the desk.

   I put my hand out.

   We shook hands.

10. I took her in my arms.

    I kissed her.

11. I tried to be businesslike.

    I couldn't.

12. I heard Mr. Spezzafly coming.

    I couldn't stop kissing Stella.

13. He left the office.

    Stella and I listened to him walking back to his office.

14. She started crying.

    I did, too.

Exercise 2

In addition to and *or* but, *other coordinating conjunctions are:* or, nor, for, so, *and* yet. *Combine each set of sentences below by using a comma and one of the following coordinating conjunctions:* and, but, or, nor, for, so, *or* yet.

EXAMPLE: I am tired.

            I am going to sleep.

           I am tired, so I am going to sleep.

1. I went to my office.

   I sat at my desk.

2. The girl in the blue dress stepped up to my desk.

   She held out a piece of folded paper to me.

(Continued on next page)

3. Stella seemed brave.

   I was scared.

4. I hardly know you.

   I know you're famous.

5. I eat my lunch in the park.

   I enjoy the fresh air.

6. I didn't leave my office at twelve o'clock.

   I had no lunch.

7. I didn't have a token.

   I didn't take the subway.

8. I left my job two months ago.

   The checks are still coming.

9. I can go to work.

   I can stay home.

10. I can go to your house.

    You can come to mine.

Exercise 3

With a partner, write a short story (one page or less) about someone's day at work or school. After you have written your paragraph, try to combine some sentences into compound sentences by using coordinating conjunctions. Read the resulting story to your classmates.

Capitalization

Every sentence begins with a capital letter. In addition, every proper noun (name of a particular person, place, or thing) begins with a capital.

In the following passages, replace lowercase letters with capital letters where needed.

there wasn't a visitor all week. friday afternoon i picked up my check and went home, and saturday morning i went up to the personnel department again, and the girl there said, "i've got a rather exciting position to offer you in the sporting goods department. mr. plattock wants a likely-looking man to demonstrate the rowing machine and the limbering-up bicycle. would you like to meet mr. plattock?"

monday i took my lunch and ate it under the fremont street ramp of the bay bridge, while mr. spezzafly ate his at his desk.

i thought about when i was eighteen and got in the marines and went to korea and got wounded and got discharged in san francisco.

Future Tense

One way to express simple future action is to use the phrase *to be going to* and the infinitive.

Exercise 1

Change the following sentences from the present to the future tense by replacing the verb with going to *and the infinitive.*

EXAMPLE: Present: I am applying for the job.

Future: **I am going to apply for the job.**

1. Clewpor is married.
2. Spezzafly opens the warehouse door.
3. Stella looks for a job.
4. Ashland tells her about his childhood.
5. The personnel director offers Ashland a new job.
6. The baby is famous.
7. No one buys any pianos.
8. I am moving the pianos again.
9. Clewpor is calling Mr. Spezzafly on the telephone.
10. The personnel manager offers him several jobs.
11. Clewpor refuses most of them.
12. He prefers to stay with Mr. Spezzafly.
13. Clewpor asks Stella to marry him.
14. They spend a great deal of money on their new house.
15. He is picking me up on his way to the office.

Exercise 2

Another way to express future action is to use the modal *will* plus the main verb. For example:

> I am / I'm going to talk to the girl in the personnel department.

> I will / I'll talk to the girl in the personnel department.

Form sentences in the future tense by choosing a main verb from the list and using will. *Use contractions. Some words may be used more than once.*

be	find	have
leave	let	make
move	try	understand
visit		

EXAMPLE: You/permitted to wear sports clothing.
        You'll be permitted to wear sports clothing.

1. You/an excellent impression.
2. If you say, "Visitor in the warehouse," I/what you're telling me.
3. You/the warehouse?
4. You/the door unlocked.
5. If someone comes in, I/you know.
6. He/not/Mr. Spezzafly.
7. His baby/famous.

Verb Tense Review

The following is a summary of Ashland's life at the time of the story. Fill in each blank with the correct form of the verb indicated. Use the simple present, present continuous, simple past, and future tenses (for future, you may use will *or* be going to*).*

When Ashland _____ young, he
                            (1. be)
_____ with various families. None of these families
        (2. live)
_____ him. At fifteen he _____ away,
        (3. adopt)   (4 . run)
and at eighteen he _____ the Marines. He
                            (5. join)
_____ in Korea, and he still _____
        (6. fight)   (7. think)
about his friends who _____ there.
                              (8. die)

Now he _____ in the piano warehouse of Sligo,
(9. work)
Baylie. He often _____ to the girl in the personnel
(10. talk)
department about other jobs, but he _____ to
(11. want)
stay in the warehouse. He _____ that he
(12. feel)
_____ to understand a lot of things. He
(13. begin)
_____ some small changes in the warehouse. He and
(14. make)
Mr. Spezzafly _____ for a visitor.
(15. wait)

Ashland _____ an ambition: to be famous. This
(16. have)
_____ his plan: Someday he _____ a
(17. be)   (18. marry)
special girl. He _____ a house. He and his wife
(19. buy)
_____ children. The entire family _____
(20. have)   (21. be)
famous to all who know them.

Word Order: Place and Time

*When using expressions which deal with time and place, the
expressions of place come before the expressions of time. Rewrite the
following sentences, placing the expressions within the parentheses
in the correct order.*

EXAMPLE: They must return their books (today—to the library).
          They must return their books to the library today.

1. Clewpor met Stella for lunch (on Tuesday—at a fancy restaurant).
2. Mr. Spezzafly left (the warehouse—a few minutes ago).
3. Mr. Spezzafly spoke on the telephone (on Tuesday—in his office).
4. We unlatched the door (to the warehouse—yesterday).
5. Ashland and Stella went (to a concert—on Thursday night).
6. That fellow goes to work with me (every morning—on the subway).
7. Ashland receives a visitor (every week—in his office).
8. Stella does her typing (in the office—every Monday).
9. Mr. Spezzafly checks the pianos (at the warehouse—once
   a month).
10. Ashland kissed Stella (in the office—last week).

*F*OLLOW UP

Topics for Discussion

1. Would you like to have Ashland's job? Why or why not?

2. If you had to advise a friend about whom to marry, which qualities would you say were important? Why?

3. If you were very wealthy, would you still want to work? Why or why not?

4. If you had time for a long lunch, what, where, and with whom would you eat?

5. Do you have a particular ambition in life? What is your ambition?

Topics for Writing

1. The woman in the personnel department is very helpful to Clewpor. In three paragraphs, describe the most helpful person you ever met and how he or she influenced your life.

2. In two paragraphs, describe the most boring or the most interesting job you ever had. What made it interesting / boring?

3. Ashland describes his unhappy childhood to Stella. Write about your childhood. Make sure to give some specific details.

4. In three paragraphs, describe how you and your wife, girlfriend, husband, boyfriend, or friend met.

5. What did Stella think about her visit to the piano warehouse? Pretend that you are Stella and write an entry in your diary or a letter to a friend about what happened on this day in your life.

Borrowing a Match

—STEPHEN LEACOCK

Borrowing a Match

◆ **PREVIEWING THE STORY**

Look at the picture, the title, and the first paragraph of the story. Answer the questions, explaining each answer.

1. Who is borrowing a match from whom?

2. What do you think the man on the left is doing? Why is he perspiring?

3. What does the man on the right seem to be thinking?

◆ **THINKING ABOUT THE TOPIC**

Think about and answer the following questions.

1. Are you embarrassed to stop strangers and ask for help? Why or why not?

2. What are some of the reasons people have stopped you on the street? What requests do they have?

3. Did you ever have problems with something like borrowing a match? What sorts of problems can occur?

You might think that borrowing a match upon the street is a simple thing. But any man who has ever tried it will assure you that it is not and will be prepared to swear on oath* to the truth of my experience of the other evening.

I was standing on the corner of the street with a cigar that I wanted to light. I had no match. I waited till a decent,[1] ordinary man came along. Then I said:

"Excuse me, sir, but could you oblige me with* the loan of a match?"

"A match?" he said, "why, certainly." Then he unbuttoned his overcoat and put his hand in the pocket of his waistcoat.[2] "I know I have one," he went on, "and I'd almost swear it's in the bottom pocket—or, hold on, though, I guess it may be in the top—just wait till I put these parcels[3] down on the sidewalk."

"Oh, don't trouble," I said, "It's really of no consequence."*

"Oh, it's no trouble, I'll have it in a minute; I know there must be one in here somewhere"—he was digging his fingers into his pockets as he spoke— "but you see this isn't the waistcoat that I generally . . . "

I saw that the man was getting excited about it. "Well, never mind," I protested;[4] "if that isn't the waistcoat that you generally—why, it doesn't matter."

"Hold on,* now, hold on!" the man said, "I've got one of the cursed[5] things in here somewhere. I guess it must be in with my watch. No, it's not there either. Wait till I try my coat. If that confounded[6] tailor only knew enough to make a pocket so that a man could get at it!"

He was getting pretty well worked up* now. He had thrown down his walking-stick and was plunging[7] at his pockets with his teeth set.* "It's that cursed young boy of mine," he hissed;[8] "this comes of his fooling[9] in my pockets. By Gad! perhaps I won't warm him up when I get home. Say, I'll bet that it's in my hip pocket. You just hold up the tail[10] of my overcoat a second till I . . . "

"No, no," I protested again, "please don't take all this trouble, it really doesn't matter. I'm sure you needn't take off your overcoat, and oh, pray don't throw away your letters and things in the snow like that, and tear out your pockets by the roots! Please, please don't trample[11] over your overcoat and put your feet through the parcels. I do hate to hear

[1] all right; nice looking

[2] vest

[3] packages

[4] objected; complained

[5] unlucky; terrible

[6] expression of disapproval

[7] digging into

[8] said in angry whisper

[9] playing

[10] end

[11] step heavily on

[12] cursing; using bad language
[13] strange
[14] high, annoying tone
[15] roughly
[16] deep noise
[17] joy
[18] inside layer of material
[19] giving way
[20] sudden wish to do something

you swearing[12] at your little boy, with that peculiar[13] whine[14] in your voice. Don't—please don't tear your clothes so savagely."[15]

Suddenly the man gave a grunt[16] of exultation,[17] and drew his hand up from inside the lining[18] of his coat.

"I've got it," he cried. "Here you are!" Then he brought it out under the light.

It was a toothpick.

Yielding[19] to the impulse[20] of the moment I pushed him under the wheels of a trolley-car and ran. ◆

IDIOMS AND PHRASES*

swear on oath	*to promise, using God's name*
to oblige (someone with)	*to do (someone) a favor; to be helpful or kind*
of no consequence	*unimportant*
hold on	*wait; be patient*
worked up	*excited*
with (his) teeth set	*in a determined way*

POST-READING

Comprehension

1. Why did the narrator want to borrow a match?

2. How did the stranger seem to the narrator when he first saw him?

3. How did the stranger respond to the narrator's request? Did he want to help?

4. What was the stranger carrying?

5. What were three reasons the stranger gave for not being able to find a match?

6. What did the narrator say when the stranger couldn't find a match? Did the stranger pay attention to the narrator?

7. What did the stranger finally produce from his pocket? What did the narrator do then?

Responding to the Story

1. Why was the narrator so angry with the stranger?

2. If you were the narrator, how would you have felt? Did you ever have an experience where someone who couldn't help you kept trying to help you?

3. What is your opinion of the stranger? Was he a "decent, ordinary" man? If so, why did he behave the way he did?

4. Do you think the narrator really pushed the man under the trolley? If no, why does he say he did?

5. If you saw this story acted out on television, do you think you would find it funnier than in writing or less funny? Explain.

VOCABULARY

Vocabulary Builder

Fill in each blank with a word from the list.

trampled	parcels	exultation
grunt	plunged	lining
peculiar	protested	swearing
savagely	tail	

1. He searched his pockets and even the _____ of his coat for the match.

2. In order to look for a match, he put his _____ down on the ground.

3. He _____ his hands into his pockets but couldn't find a match.

4. The narrator _____, "Please don't bother to look for a match."

5. While looking for a match, he accidentally _____ on the parcels which were on the ground.

6. He tore _____ at his clothes.

7. He began _____ at his tailor and his child, who in no way were to blame.

8. The narrator held up the _____ of the stranger's coat.

(Continued on next page)

9. At first the stranger seemed ordinary, but by this time he seemed quite _____.

10. He gave a _____ of _____ when he thought he had found a match.

Idiom Exercise

Choose the answer that means the same as the underlined idiom in the sentence.

1. Can you <u>oblige me</u> and hold these parcels for a moment?
   a. answer a question for me   c. give me some help
   b. listen to me   d. wait for me

2. The stranger was getting very <u>worked up</u> about not finding a match.
   a. excited   c. peculiar
   b. unhappy   d. unpleasant

3. <u>Teeth set</u>, he continued to empty his pockets.
   a. chewing   c. while talking
   b. crying   d. in a determined way

4. The request was really <u>of no consequence</u>.
   a. terrible   c. interesting
   b. unimportant   d. unusual

5. Do you <u>swear on oath</u> that the story is true?
   a. realize   c. prefer
   b. promise seriously d. feel strongly

Word Forms

Fill in the correct word form from those listed. Each form should be used.

1. borrow, borrower, borrowing
   a. Did you _____ cigarettes from him?
   b. Shakespeare said, "Neither a lender nor a _____ be."
   c. My friends are always _____ matches from me.

2. assuring, assurance, assured
   a. She kept _____ me that there wasn't a problem.
   b. I had his _____ that my overcoat would be ready by tomorrow.
   c. The boy _____ his father that he had not taken the matches.

3. oblige, obliging, obligation, obligatory

    a. You have an _____ to give him a match.

    b. It is _____ to wear a jacket in certain restaurants.

    c. Please _____ me by giving me a cigarette.

    d. He was very _____ about sharing his matches.

*S*TRUCTURE

Quotation Marks

Use quotations to set off the exact words of speakers. Periods, commas, and other punctuation marks go inside the quotation marks.

In the following passage, put quotation marks where you think they are needed.

As I was walking down the street on a very cold snowy night, a man approached me and said, Could you please give me a match?

I looked at the man carefully. He was wearing black pants, a black hat, and black gloves. Something about him frightened me. Again he asked me to give him a match. As I reached into my pocket, he said, Please hurry. I'm very cold.

I'm doing the best I can, I answered. My hands were shaking. I wanted to tell him that I had no matches. However, I set my teeth, reached into my pocket, and gave him my lighter.

After he lit his cigarette, he returned my lighter and said with a smile, Thank you. I was afraid to ask a stranger for a match, but I wanted to smoke so badly that I overcame my fears. Have a good evening.

Expressing Uncertainty

There are various ways to express uncertainty. For example, if you are not sure someone has a match, instead of saying *He has a match*, you can use an additional verb such as *think* or *guess:*

    I think/guess (that) he has a match.

Or you can add a modal, such as *may, must, should, might,* or *could:*

    He must have a match.
    He should have a match.
    He might/could/may have a match.

(Continued on next page)

(*Must* means almost sure; *should* means quite sure; and *may, might,* and *could* mean not at all sure.) You can use both these ways of expressing uncertainty together; for example, *I think I might have a match.*

Exercise 1

Change the sentences to sentences expressing uncertainty, using the words indicated.

EXAMPLE: Borrowing a match is simple. (think)
I think borrowing a match is simple.

1. I have a match. (think)
2. It is in the top pocket. (guess/may)
3. There is one in here somewhere. (must)
4. It is in with my watch. (guess/must)
5. It's in my hip pocket. (think)
6. It is in the bottom pocket. (guess/could)
7. It is in the overcoat lining. (might)

Exercise 2

With a partner, play a guessing game. Pick any noun in the story. Write a blank for each letter in the word. For example, if your word is match, *write* _ _ _ _ _ . *Your partner must guess the word by guessing its letters. For example, your partner may say, "I think the word has an* a" *or "There could be an* a." *If the guess is correct, write the letter in the space(s) where it goes. Keep track of the number of guesses. When your partner knows the word, he or she says, "That word must be* match." *Then your partner picks a noun. The person who figures out the word in fewer guesses wins. In guessing, be sure to use the modals* could *and* might, should, *and* must (*depending on how sure you are about your guesses*).

Imperatives

Imperatives are used to ask someone to do something or to not do something; for example, *Wait till I put these parcels down on the sidewalk.* The subject of an imperative does not occur in the actual sentence and is understood to be *you.* Imperatives can be made more polite by the addition of *please: Please don't take all this trouble.*

Exercise 1

Reread the story to identify imperatives. Write down some imperatives from the story.

1.

2.

3.

4.

5.

Exercise 2

Imperatives are often used in giving directions or instructions. Write some instructions telling people how to do something that you know how to do—for example, how to prepare a certain meal, play a certain game, or use a certain machine. In your instructions, use imperatives, including some imperatives with don't.

This/That; These/Those

We use *this* to show that something is nearby; we use *that* to show that something is at a distance. *These* is the plural of *this. Those* is the plural of *that.*

Fill in each blank with this, that, these, *or* those.

EXAMPLE: _____*This*_____ cigar in my hand is not lit.

1. I'm sorry to trouble you—I see you are carrying all _____ parcels.

2. It's no trouble—let me just put _____ parcels down.

3. Wait till I put _____ walking stick down, too.

4. I'm sure I have a match in one of the pockets of _____ waistcoat, but _____ pockets are annoying.

5. _____ confounded tailor I use doesn't know how to sew pockets.

6. _____ confounded son of mine must have been fooling around in my pockets; when I get home, I'll warm him!

7. Don't trouble yourself; it might be easier if I try to get a match from _____ people over there.

8. I found it! Here you are! You can use _____ match.

9. _____ "match" that you're holding happens to be a toothpick.

There Is / There Are

There is a word used to introduce a sentence. The verb agrees with the subject which follows the verb when *there* is used to start the sentence. *There* is never used as the subject of a sentence.

Exercise 1

Fill in the blank with is *or* are *in the following sentences.*

Example: There _____ *is* _____ only one cigar in my pocket.

There _____ *are* _____ many cigars in his pocket.

1. There _____ many pockets in my overcoat.
2. There _____ no clear answer to this question.
3. _____ there any lessons that the narrator can learn from this experience?
4. There _____ a good tailor around the corner.
5. There _____ a book of matches on the floor.

Exercise 2

Make up five sentences of your own, using there is *or* there are. *Make sure that the subject agrees with the verb.*

Possessive Pronouns

The following sentences show possession. Fill in the blank in the second sentence of each pair with the correct possessive pronoun.

Example: Have you seen Jack's jacket?
Have you seen his jacket?

That wallet is Joan's.
That wallet is hers.

1. These parcels belong to my son and me.
   These parcels are _____ .

2. Is this your pack of cigarettes?
   This pack is _____ .

3. He had matches in the pockets of his coat.
   _____ matches were in _____ pockets.

4. That overcoat belongs to him.
   That overcoat is _____ .

5. The man has many toothpicks.
   Those toothpicks are _____ .

6. Those watches belong to the stranger and his son.
   Those watches are _____ .

7. Come look at my new suit.
   This suit is _____ .

8. We picked up our letters.
   Those letters are _____ .

9. I asked the children to clean up their room.
   That dirty room is _____ .

10. Have you been smoking cigars?
    Those cigars are _____ .

Present Continuous Review

The present continuous tense is used to show an action that is happening at the present moment. To form the present continuous tense, we use the present tense of the verb *to be* and the present participle (*-ing* form) of the main verb.

Change the verbs in the sentences below from simple present to present continuous form. Make any other necessary changes.

EXAMPLE: She smokes a cigarette every day.
          She is smoking a cigarette now.

1. He wears a dark suit.
2. He often walks in the park.
3. He often carries a walking stick in his right hand.
4. He always borrows matches from his friends.
5. He always takes the trouble to help a stranger.
6. He often brings his son candy.
7. The tailor often calls me to come in for a fitting.
8. I try to quit smoking every day.
9. My son always takes things from my pockets.
10. I always look for matches in my jacket pockets.

ROLE PLAY: With a classmate, act out a scene similar to the one in the story. One person is getting angry because he/she cannot find what he/she is looking for, and the other person is trying to calm him/her down.

Use the present continuous tense as often as possible.

FOLLOW UP

Topics for Discussion

1. Think back to a time when you were lost or needed directions. How did you decide whom to ask?

2. When a stranger asks you for (a) directions, (b) a match, or (c) change for a dollar, how do you react? Why?

3. When you become frustrated, how do you usually react? Do you get upset, like the stranger, or do you remain calm?

4. The stranger keeps blaming other people—his tailor, his son—for his problems. Do you know people who tend to blame others? Why do people do this?

5. The narrator's opinion of the stranger changes quickly. Have you met anyone who seemed one way when you first saw him or her but soon seemed very different? If so, describe.

Topics for Writing

1. Did you ever misplace anything important? How did you go about looking for it? Write a paragraph describing your search and your feelings.

2. In this story both characters become very angry with other people. Write a two-paragraph essay describing how you act when you are angry with someone.

3. The stranger tried to help but failed. Write a paragraph describing a time when you wanted to help someone but failed, or wanted to help someone and were able to.

4. In this story, the narrator pushes the stranger under the wheels of a trolley car. Write another ending to the story.

5. In this story, something that seems simple becomes very difficult and can't be done. Write a short story about something else that seems simple but turns out to be difficult or impossible. You can base the story on an experience you had or make it up.

The Private Life
of Mr. Bidwell

—JAMES THURBER

The Private Life of Mr. Bidwell

♦ ## PREVIEWING THE STORY

*Look at the picture, the title, and the first paragraph of the
story. Answer the questions, explaining each answer.*

1. What is the relationship between the man and the woman in the
   picture? What kind of mood do they seem to be in?

2. What do you think George might be "up to"?

3. What do you think "Private Life" in the title might mean?

♦ ## THINKING ABOUT THE TOPIC

Think about and answer the following questions.

1. What are some reasons why a marriage might be unhappy?

2. How might a long-married couple who are unhappy treat
   each other?

3. Think of another country. What are the traditional responsibilities
   of the wife? The husband?

F rom where she was sitting, Mrs. Bidwell could not see her husband, but she had a curious[1] feeling of tension:[2] she knew he was up to something.*

"What are you doing, George?" she demanded, her eyes still on her book.

"Mm?"

"What's the matter* with you?"

"Pahhhhh-h-h," said Mr. Bidwell, in a long, pleasurable exhale.[3] "I was holding my breath."

Mrs. Bidwell twisted creakingly in her chair and looked at him; he was sitting behind her in his favorite place under the parchment lamp with the street scene of old New York on it. "I was just holding my breath," he said again.

"Well, please don't do it," said Mrs. Bidwell, and went back to her book. There was silence for five minutes.

"George!" said Mrs. Bidwell.

"Bwaaaaaa," said Mr. Bidwell. "What?"

"Will you please *stop* that?" she said. "It makes me nervous."

"I don't see how that bothers you," he said. "Can't I breathe?"

"You can breathe without holding your breath like a goop," said Mrs. Bidwell. "Goop" was a word that she was fond of using; she rather lazily applied it to everything. It annoyed Mr. Bidwell.

"Deep breathing," said Mr. Bidwell, in the impatient tone he used when explaining anything to his wife, "is good exercise. You ought to take more exercise."

"Well, please don't do it around me," said Mrs. Bidwell, turning again to the pages of Mr. Galsworthy.[4]

At the Cowan's party, a week later, the room was full of chattering people when Mrs. Bidwell, who was talking to Lida Carroll, suddenly turned around as if she had been summoned.[5] In a chair in a far corner of the room, Mr. Bidwell was holding his breath. His chest was expanded, his chin drawn in; there was a strange stare in his eyes, and his face was slightly empurpled. Mrs. Bidwell moved into the line of his vision and gave him a sharp, penetrating[6] look. He deflated[7] slowly and looked away.

---

[1] strange
[2] mental strain
[3] breathing out
[4] a writer of fiction
[5] called
[6] deep
[7] let out air

85

Later, in the car, after they had driven in silence a mile or more on the way home, Mrs. Bidwell said, "It seems to me you might at least have the kindness not to hold your breath in other people's houses."

"It wasn't hurting anybody," said Mr. Bidwell.

"You looked silly!" said his wife. "You looked perfectly crazy!" She was driving and began to speed up,* as she always did when excited or angry. "What do you suppose people thought—you sitting there all swelled up,[8] with your eyes popping out?"

[8] big and round

"I wasn't all swelled up," he said, angrily.

"You looked like a goop," she said. The car slowed down, sighed, and came to a complete, despondent[9] stop.

[9] very unhappy

"We're out of gas," said Mrs. Bidwell. It was bitterly cold and nastily sleeting.[10] Mr. Bidwell took a long, deep breath.

[10] mix of rain and snow

The breathing situation in the Bidwell family reached a critical point when Mr. Bidwell began to inhale[11] in his sleep, slowly, and exhale with a protracted,[12] growling "woooooooo." Mrs. Bidwell, ordinarily a sound sleeper (except on nights when she was sure burglars[13] were getting in), would wake up and reach over and shake her husband. "George!" she would say.

[11] breathe in
[12] taking a long time
[13] robbers

"Hawwwwwww," Mr. Bidwell would say, thickly. "Wahs maa nah, hm?"

After he had turned over and gone back to sleep, Mrs. Bidwell would lie awake, thinking.

One morning at breakfast she said, "George, I'm not going to put up with* this another day. If you can't stop blowing up like a grampus, I'm going to leave you." There was a slight, quick lift in Mr. Bidwell's heart, but he tried to look surprised and hurt.

"All right," he said. "Let's not talk about it."

Mrs. Bidwell buttered another piece of toast. She described to him the way he sounded in his sleep. He read the paper.

[14] filling up with air

With considerable effort, Mr. Bidwell kept from inflating[14] his chest for about a week, but one night at the McNallys' he hit on the idea of seeing how many seconds he could hold his breath. He was rather bored by the McNallys' party, anyway. He began timing himself with his wristwatch in a remote[15] corner of the living-room. Mrs. Bidwell, who was in the kitchen talking children and clothes with Bea McNally, left her abruptly and slipped back into the living-room. She stood quietly behind

[15] far away

her husband's chair. He knew she was there, and tried to let out his breath imperceptibly.[16]

"I see you," she said, in a low, cold tone. Mr. Bidwell jumped up.

"Why don't you leave me alone?" he demanded.

"Will you please lower your voice?" she said, smiling so that if anyone were looking he wouldn't think the Bidwells were arguing.

"I'm getting pretty damned tired of this," said Bidwell in a low voice.

"You've ruined my evening!" she whispered.

"You've ruined mine, too!" he whispered back. They knifed each other, from head to stomach, with their eyes.

"Sitting here like a goop, holding your breath," said Mrs. Bidwell. "People will think you are an idiot." She laughed, turning to greet a lady who was approaching them.

Mr. Bidwell sat in his office the next afternoon, a black, moist[17] afternoon, tapping a pencil on his desk, and scowling.[18] "All right, then, get out, get out!" he muttered. "What do I care?" He was visualizing[19] the scene when Mrs. Bidwell would walk out on him. After going through it several times, he returned to his work, feeling vaguely[20] contented.[21] He made up his mind to breathe any way he wanted to, no matter what she did. And, having come to this decision, he oddly enough, and quite without effort, lost interest in holding his breath.

Everything went rather smoothly at the Bidwells' for a month or so. Mr. Bidwell didn't do anything to annoy his wife beyond leaving his razor on her dressing-table and forgetting to turn out the hall light when he went to bed. Then there came the night of the Bentons' party.

Mr. Bidwell, bored as usual, was sitting in a far corner of the room, breathing normally. His wife was talking animatedly[22] with Beth Williamson about negligees.[23] Suddenly her voice slowed and an uneasy look came into her eyes: George was up to something. She turned around and sought him out.* To anyone but Mrs. Bidwell he must have seemed like any husband sitting in a chair. But his wife's lips set tightly. She walked casually over to him.

"What are you doing?" she demanded.

"Hm?" he said, looking at her vacantly.[24]

---

[16] unnoticeably
[17] wet
[18] making an angry face
[19] seeing in his mind
[20] not strongly
[21] happy, satisfied
[22] excitedly, with feeling
[23] women's fancy nightgowns
[24] not seeing or paying attention

[25] poisonous

[26] made longer in time

[27] searching, examining carefully

[28] clear, easily understood

[29] ability to put up with

[30] criticize strongly

[31] stopping and starting

[32] walk

"What are you doing?" she demanded, again. He gave her a harsh, venomous[25] look, which she returned.

"I'm multiplying numbers in my head," he said, slowly and evenly, "if you must know." In the prolonged,[26] probing[27] examination that they silently, without moving any muscles save those of their eyes, gave each other, it became solidly, frozenly apparent[28] to both of them that the end of their endurance[29] had arrived. The curious bond that held them together snapped—rather more easily than either had supposed was possible. That night, while undressing for bed, Mr. Bidwell calmly multiplied numbers in his head. Mrs. Bidwell stared coldly at him for a few moments, holding a stocking in her hand; she didn't bother to berate[30] him. He paid no attention to her. The thing was simply over.

George Bidwell lives alone now (his wife remarried). He never goes to parties any more, and his old circle of friends rarely sees him. The last time that any of them did see him, he was walking along a country road with the halting,[31] uncertain gait[32] of a blind man: he was trying to see how many steps he could take without opening his eyes. ◆

IDIOMS AND PHRASES*

be up to something	*be doing something (often something not good)*
be the matter	*be the problem*
speed up	*to go faster*
put up with	*suffer patiently*
to seek (someone) out (past tense: sought him out)	*to look for*

POST-**READING**

Comprehension

Complete the sentences by circling a, b, *or* c.

1. At the beginning of the story, what Mr. Bidwell was up to was
   a. criticizing Mrs. Bidwell.
   b. being rude to guests at a party.
   c. holding his breath.

2. The car came to a stop because
   a. it was out of gas.
   b. it was too cold outside.
   c. Mrs. Bidwell was paying more attention to arguing than to driving.

3. The breathing situation became serious when
   a. Mr. Bidwell began to hold his breath in his sleep.
   b. Mrs. Bidwell called her husband a "goop."
   c. Mr. Bidwell turned purple.

4. Mr. Bidwell turned from holding his breath to
   a. leaving his things around the house.
   b. multiplying numbers in his head.
   c. walking around with his eyes closed.

5. At the end of the story,
   a. George Bidwell lives alone, but his wife has remarried.
   b. both George Bidwell and his wife have remarried.
   c. George Bidwell and his wife might get back together again.

6. Mrs. Bidwell smiles even when they're arguing because
   a. she wants to make a good impression.
   b. she's very friendly.
   c. she likes to fight.

7. When the Bidwells "knifed each other from head to stomach, with their eyes," they were
   a. physically harming each other.
   b. looking at each other with hatred.
   c. playing a game.

Responding to the Story

1. Why does Mr. Bidwell's breathing bother Mrs. Bidwell? Why is she so annoyed by her husband's actions in other people's houses even when no one else notices them?

2. Why do you think Mr. Bidwell does the things he does?

3. Why don't Mr. and Mrs. Bidwell get along? How would you describe each of them? How do they differ from each other?

4. According to the story, who seems to be more responsible for the fighting? Why?

5. Based on the story, what do you think is Mr. Bidwell's opinion of women? Of people in general?

6. Why does Mr. Bidwell lose interest in holding his breath once he decides he can breathe any way he wants to?

7. Now that you've read the story, what meanings do you think "private life" in the title has?

8. Do you think Mr. Bidwell and his wife are each happy at the end of the story? Why or why not?

 **V**OCABULARY

Vocabulary Builder

Answer yes *or* no *to each of the following questions. Give reasons for your answers.*

1. When there is *tension* between Mr. and Mrs. Bidwell, are they getting along well with each other?

2. When Mrs. Bidwell makes a *venomous* remark to Mr. Bidwell, is she being nice to him?

3. Was Mr. Bidwell *scowling* because he was thinking happy thoughts?

4. If the Bidwells had *prolonged* their marriage, would they have stayed together for a longer period of time?

5. Is a person likely to see more with a *penetrating* look than with a *vacant* look?

6. Was Mr. Bidwell *despondent* when his marriage ended?

7. Do you think that the divorce proceedings between Mr. and Mrs. Bidwell were *protracted*?

8. When Mr. Bidwell *visualized* Mrs. Bidwell walking out on him, was she actually doing it?

9. Does Mrs. Bidwell *berate* her husband when she is angry with him?

10. At the end of the story, was the *bond* between Mr. and Mrs. Bidwell strong?

Idiom Exercise

Use each of the underlined idioms in another sentence, following the suggested pattern.

EXAMPLE: Mrs. Bidwell began to <u>speed up</u> because she was angry.

I tried to speed up because I wanted to pass that other car.

1. Because he was so quiet, Mrs. Bidwell knew her husband was <u>up to something</u>.
   Because _____ up to something.

2. She will have to <u>put up with</u> him until she gets a divorce.
   _____ put up with _____ until _____ .

3. Mr. Bidwell may be holding his breath, but <u>there is nothing the matter</u> with his lungs.
   _____ , but there is nothing the matter _____ .

Say It Right

How many of these words can you pronounce correctly? Try them and see.

1. creakingly KREEK ing lee
2. summon SUHM in
3. penetrating PEN i trayt ing
4. deflated di FLAYT id
5. protracted proh TRAKT id
6. scowling SKOWL ing
7. sought SAWT
8. negligees NEG li zhayz
9. venomous VEN uhm uhs
10. halting HAWLT ing
11. berate buh RAYT
12. stared STAYRD

STRUCTURE

Prepositions

Exercise 1

Complete the following paragraph with the correct prepositions from the box. Each preposition should be used at least once.

at	behind	in	into	of	on	out	with

One night _____ the McNallys' he hit
(1)
_____ the idea _____ seeing how
(2)   (3)
many seconds he could hold his breath. He began timing himself
_____ his wrist-watch _____ a remote
(4)   (5)
corner _____ the living-room. Mrs. Bidwell, who was
(6)
_____ the kitchen talking children and clothes
(7)
_____ Bea McNally, left her abruptly and slipped
(8)
back _____ the living-room. She stood quietly
(9)
_____ her husband's chair. He knew she was there, and
(10)
tried to let _____ his breath imperceptibly.
(11)

Exercise 2

Below is a list of the most frequently used prepositions. With a partner, make up and write a one-paragraph scene between Mr. and Mrs. Bidwell—at home, at a party, or elsewhere. Use at least ten of the prepositions in the list. (You can use these prepositions as many times as you want.) Read your paragraph to your classmates.

about	above	across
after	against	among
at	before	behind
below	between	by
down	during	for
from	in	into

of	off	on
over	past	since
through	under	to
towards	until	up
with	within	without

Contractions

Contractions, or shortened forms, are especially common in spoken English. In writing contractions, an apostrophe is used to show that one or more letters have been left out. Rewrite each sentence so that it includes one contraction.

EXAMPLE: From where she was sitting, Mrs. Bidwell could not see her husband.

From where she was sitting, Mrs. Bidwell couldn't see her husband.

1. "What is the matter with you?" she demanded.
2. "Can I not breathe?" Mr. Bidwell asked.
3. "Please do not do it," Mrs. Bidwell said.
4. She suddenly turned around as if she had been summoned.
5. "It was not hurting anybody," said Mr. Bidwell.
6. "We are out of gas," said Mrs. Bidwell.
7. One morning, she said, "George, I am not going to put up with this another day."
8. "All right," he said. "Let us not think about it."
9. She smiled so that if anyone were looking he would not think the Bidwells were arguing.
10. "They will think you are an idiot," she said.
11. "I am getting pretty damned tired of this," he said.
12. "You have ruined my evening," she said.

Past Continuous Tense

The past continuous tense is formed with the past tense of the verb *to be* and the present participle (*-ing* form) of the main verb. The past continuous is used to talk about something that was going on or continuing at some definite time in the past. The past continuous is used with the simple past to describe something continuing that was interrupted by an action. The interrupting action is expressed in the simple past. For example: *Mr. Bidwell was holding his breath when Mrs. Bidwell walked into the room.*

(Continued on next page)

Exercise 1

Complete each sentence by forming the past continuous tense with the verb indicated.

EXAMPLE: From where she _____*was sitting*_____, Mrs. Bidwell could
(sit)

not see her husband.

1. Mr. Bidwell _____ behind her in his favorite
(sit)
place under the parchment lamp.

2. "It _____ anybody," said Mr. Bidwell.
(not/hurt)

3. Mr. Bidwell _____ the scene when Mrs. Bidwell
(visualize)
would walk out on him.

4. Mrs. Bidwell _____ animatedly about negligees.
(talk)

5. That night, while Mr. Bidwell _____ for bed, he
(undress)
multiplied numbers in his head.

6. Mrs. Bidwell, who _____ a stocking in her hand,
(hold)
stared coldly at him.

Exercise 2

Fill in each blank with the past continuous or the simple past form of the verb indicated.

EXAMPLE: When Mrs. Bidwell _____*walked*_____ into the
(walk)
room, he _____*was holding*_____ his breath.
(hold)

At the Cowans' party, the room was full of chattering people when

Mrs. Bidwell, who _____ to Lida Carroll, suddenly
(1. talk)

_____ around. In a far corner of the room she
(2. turn)

_____ Mr. Bidwell. He _____ his breath.
(3. see)   (4. hold)

They had an argument on the way home, when Mrs. Bidwell

_____. But then the car _____ down,
(5. drive)   (6. slow)

_____, and _____ to a stop.
(7. sigh)   (8. come)

The last time that any of his old friends _____ him,
(9. see)
he _____ along a country road, with the halting,
(10. walk)
uncertain gait of a blind man: he _____ to see how many
(11. try)
steps he could take without opening his eyes.

Past Perfect Tense

The past perfect tense expresses a past time that comes before another past time. It is formed by using the simple past in one part of the sentence, and the past tense of to have *with the past participle of the main verb. Supply the past perfect tense for the sentences below.*

EXAMPLE: He thought he _____*had left*_____ his wrist-watch at home.
(leave)

1. When Mrs. Bidwell saw her husband, she could see that he

   _____ up to something. When she questioned
   (be)
   him, he said that he _____ anything wrong.
   (not do)

2. She suspected that he _____ on the couch for
   (sit)
   five minutes holding his breath.

3. After he _____ over and _____
   (turn)   (go)
   back to sleep, Mrs. Bidwell lay awake, thinking.

4. After the Bidwells left our house, we never bothered to ask if they

   _____ arguing.
   (stop)

5. She thought that he _____ breathing.
   (stop)

6. The judge summoned them to court after they _____
   (file)
   for divorce.

7. Mr. Bidwell was very happy when he learned that his wife

   _____.
   (remarry)

8. After they _____ a few miles, Mr. Bidwell started
   (drive)
   counting numbers in his head again.

(Continued on next page)

9. Mrs. Bidwell did not realize how much she

_____ him with her nasty remarks.
   (hurt)
10. Although she _____ him not to embarrass her in
      (tell)
    public, he continued to speak in a loud voice.

Adjectives and Adverbs

*Change each sentence with an adverb into a similar sentence with
an adjective, and change each sentence with an adjective into a
similar sentence with an adverb. Remember that adjectives modify
nouns and adverbs modify verbs. (Most sentences can be changed in
more than one way.)*

EXAMPLES: "Pahhhhh-h-h," said Mr. Bidwell, in a pleasurable exhale.
        "Pahhhhh-h-h," said Mr. Bidwell, exhaling pleasurably.

     Mrs. Bidwell lazily applied "goop" to everything.
     Mrs. Bidwell was lazy and applied "goop" to everything.

1. Mrs. Bidwell gave him a penetrating look.
2. The car came to a despondent stop.
3. Mrs. Bidwell was a sound sleeper.
4. "Hawwwwww," Mr. Bidwell would say, thickly.
5. There was a slight lift in Mr. Bidwell's heart.
6. She stood quietly behind his chair.
7. He tried to let out his breath imperceptibly.
8. "I see you," she said in a cold tone.
9. Everything went in a smooth way for a month or so.
10. He gave her a venomous look.

Would in Past Time

Would can be used to express actions that happened repeatedly or
habitually in the past. For example, *Mr. Bidwell would annoy his wife,
and Mrs. Bidwell would berate her husband* means that the actions of
annoying and berating happened often.

Exercise 1

In the following description, change the verbs in the simple past into structures with would. *What is the difference in meaning?*

Mrs. Bidwell, ordinarily a sound sleeper, woke up and shook her husband. "George!" she said.

"Hawwwwww," Mr. Bidwell said, thickly. "Wahs maa nah, hm?"

After he had turned over and gone back to sleep, Mrs. Bidwell lay awake, thinking.

Exercise 2

Write a short paragraph about something you and your family did repeatedly when you were a child (for example, something you often did on weekends, somewhere you often went during the summer). Use would *in your paragraph.*

 **F**OLLOW **U**P

Topics for Discussion

1. Do you think this is a typical husband-wife relationship? Why or why not?

2. How can you tell when someone is unhappily married? Are couples often able to hide their unhappiness from friends, as Mrs. Bidwell tries to do?

3. Mr. and Mrs. Bidwell obviously have been married for a long time. Why do so many marriages that are unhappy nevertheless last a long time?

4. Do you think that for a marriage to be happy it is important that the husband and wife have a lot in common? Why or why not?

5. Mr. Bidwell annoys his wife with his bad habits. What are some small bad habits that annoy you the most?

6. Pretend you are Mrs. Bidwell. In a three- to five-minute presentation, describe your problems with your husband.

Topics for Writing

1. Write two paragraphs explaining why so many couples get divorced today.

2. Did you ever have an unhappy relationship which you tried to improve? List some of the steps you took to improve the relationship.

3. Write two paragraphs telling what would make you unhappy in a marriage.

4. In a paragraph, describe what Mr. and Mrs. Bidwell are really fighting about.

5. George Bidwell holds his breath, multiplies numbers in his head, and walks with his eyes closed. What else might he think of to do? Write a short story that takes place after his wife leaves, in which he tries something else. What happens? Your story can be funny or serious.

6. Suppose Mrs. Bidwell wrote you a letter asking for your advice on how to save her marriage. In a three-paragraph letter, give her your best advice.

The Prize Fish

—Jack Scott

The Prize Fish

◆ **PREVIEWING THE STORY**

Look at the picture, the title, and the first paragraph of the story. Answer the questions, explaining each answer.

1. What does the author mean by "prize" fish?

2. Describe the fish in the picture. Where do you think this fish is?

3. What do you think might happen in the story?

◆ **THINKING ABOUT THE TOPIC**

Think about and answer the following questions.

1. What are some of the pleasures of fishing?

2. Think of a country other than the United States. What are some of the most popular pets to keep at home?

3. Do you think that a fish could be an interesting pet? Why?

4. Did you ever enter a contest? If so, how important was it to you to win the contest? Is it ever acceptable to cheat in order to win?

H enry Pludge had a fool proof[1] plan to win the fishing derby.[2] It was ludicrously[3] simple. He decided that he would catch a salmon, keep it alive in a tank in his basement, fatten it up* for a year, and walk away with the first prize.

Henry built a large steel tank in his basement, swore his wife to secrecy,* and went fishing. After several days he landed a small, eight-pound spring salmon. He kept it alive in a large washtub which he carried to his home under the cloak of darkness.* He dumped[4] the salmon into the tank, started the system of constantly changing water, and went upstairs to bed.

For the first few days it was touch and go* with the fish. He was finding the change from salt to fresh water too sudden. He sulked[5] unhappily in one corner of the tank, looking up at Henry with brooding,[6] baleful[7] eyes. What's more, the salmon refused to eat and began wasting away.* Once, when Henry dangled a fresh herring[8] in front of his nose, the salmon wheeled[9] and bit Henry sharply on the wrist. Henry cursed the fish and shook his fist at the tank. "It'll be a pleasure to conk[10] you come next August," he cried.

The next morning when he returned to the tank, the herring was gone. The salmon was finning[11] at the surface, obviously looking for breakfast.

Once the salmon started eating he proved to be a glutton.[12] Henry soon discovered that the fish would eat almost anything. He was looking into the tank one day, munching on an apple, when he dropped the core.[13] The salmon took it at a gulp.[14]

The fish proved more than cooperative[15] with Henry's plan to force-feed it. It ate watermelon, corn-on-the-cob, hash,[16] cigarette butts, cheese and crackers, chile con carne, and several other unlikely items including roast beef, which it preferred well done.*

Henry began spending more and more time in the basement. He liked to watch the salmon making its swift, effortless circles in the tank. He had taken to calling it "Sam" and sometimes he caught himself talking to it, as men talk to dogs.

[1] that can't fail

[2] contest

[3] ridiculously

[4] threw in

[5] showed anger through silence

[6] sad

[7] angry, hating, evil

[8] a kind of fish

[9] turned around quickly

[10] hit hard on head (colloq.)

[11] moving his fins

[12] a greedy eater

[13] tough center part

[14] quick swallow

[15] helpful

[16] chopped, recooked meat

¹⁷ warm liking

¹⁸ moved back and forth

¹⁹ got used to

²⁰ moved quickly

²¹ jumping into the air

²² hitting

²³ container with wood dust

²⁴ very large; amazing

²⁵ pointer (on a machine)

²⁶ beginning of day

²⁷ alone; by itself

²⁸ small body of water

²⁹ body of water

³⁰ put food on a fishing hook

³¹ hard part of the head

³² throw out; get rid of

³³ very large

³⁴ kill; send away

³⁵ looked

³⁶ taken away, refused to give

³⁷ turned

³⁸ loud sound made by water falling

³⁹ very large

⁴⁰ slowly in time

⁴¹ curving

⁴² good-bye

Sam the Salmon responded to this affection.[17] When Henry spoke to him by name he answered with bubbles. His powerful tail wagged[18] whenever Pludge's face appeared over the rim of the tank.

Like a goldfish in a small bowl, Sam adapted[19] himself to his close quarters and, though he grew bigger by the day, he appeared to be getting enough exercise. He looped and circled, darted[20] in swift triangles.

It was only in the spring that he appeared unhappy, and the sound of him leaping[21] and slapping[22] the surface kept the Pludges awake many nights. Once they had to go down and carry him back to the tank from the sawdust bin[23] where a prodigious[24] leap had carried him.

"The poor fish is probably wanting a mate," Henry said to his wife.

"So will I if you stay in this basement much longer," his wife replied.

On the morning of the great fishing derby Henry put Sam on the scales and watched the indicator[25] go up to sixty-four pounds, eight ounces. "Wow!" he exclaimed. Sam wagged his tail.

In the dawn[26] Henry placed Sam in a smaller tank, drove to an isolated[27] cove[28] and loaded the tank into a rowboat. Then he headed out* into the sound.[29] The plan was simple. He would bait[30] a hook with fresh herring. Poor, trusting Sam would take it. Then Henry would conk him on the skull,[31] jettison[32] the smaller tank, and go in to claim his reward.

Far out in the sound Henry shipped his oars, carefully readied the gigantic[33] club with which to dispatch[34] Sam, and began to bait the hook. Sam rose to the surface and peered[35] over the rim of the tank, his tail wagging eagerly.

Henry's hands fumbled with the herring. "The poor fish," he was thinking to himself. "I have denied[36] him a whole year of freedom, kept him locked in a basement far from deep water and girl salmon and now ... now I am going to kill him when he trusts me." His eyes clouded over. His lips began to tremble. Sam looked at him inquiringly.

Suddenly Henry Pludge lifted the tank with a mighty effort and tipped[37] it over the side. There was a great splash[38] and Sam appeared at the surface, shaking his massive[39] head. He began to swim in small circles, as if in the basement tank, but gradually[40] they widened out until Henry lost sight of him. Then far out now, Sam leaped joyously, his great silver body arching[41] above the water.

"Farewell,[42] Sam," Henry shouted. Then the fish was gone. ◆

IDIOMS AND PHRASES*

fatten up	*to feed (someone or something) a lot*
swear to secrecy	*make (someone) promise not to tell*
under the cloak of darkness	*in the dark*
touch and go	*very uncertain*
wasting away	*becoming thinner every day*
well done	*cooked for a long time*
headed out	*went away*

POST-READING

Comprehension

1. Why did Henry bring the salmon home?
2. Describe Sam's behavior when Henry brought him home.
3. Why did Henry give the salmon so much food?
4. What are some of the foods that Henry fed the salmon?
5. After a while, how did Sam seem to feel about being in Henry's house? How did Henry feel about Sam?
6. How did Henry's wife feel about the salmon? Why?
7. When did Sam become unhappy? Why did he become unhappy?
8. What was Henry's plan on the day of the derby? Why didn't he carry out his plan?
9. How did Sam respond when he was set free?

Responding to the Story

1. Why did Henry's attitude toward the salmon change?
2. Based on the story, what is your opinion of Henry? Explain.
3. Was Henry mistreating Sam? Why or why not?
4. What is unexpected and humorous about Sam?
5. Now that you've read the story, in what way is Sam a "prize fish"?
6. After this experience with Sam, do you think Henry will continue to go fishing? Why or why not?

VOCABULARY

Vocabulary Builder

Replace the underlined word or words in each sentence with a word from the list.

leap	glutton	dawn
rim	gradually	bin
gulp	core	skull
affection	adapted	

1. Once Sam started eating, he proved to be a <u>greedy eater</u>.
2. Sam ate the <u>tough center part</u> of an apple with a <u>quick swallow</u>.
3. Sam wagged his tail whenever Pludge's face appeared over the <u>edge</u> of the tank.
4. Like a goldfish in a small bowl, Sam <u>got used</u> to his living space.
5. He responded to the <u>warm liking</u> Henry showed him.
6. The Pludges kept a sawdust <u>container</u> in the basement.
7. Sam made a prodigious <u>jump</u> out of his tank.
8. At <u>daybreak</u>, Henry placed Sam in a smaller tank.
9. Sam almost got his <u>hard part of the head</u> cracked.
10. When Henry let him go, Sam swam <u>slowly</u> away.

Idiom Exercise

Write your own sentences using each of the idiomatic expressions listed.

EXAMPLE: fatten up

When I was a child, my mother thought I was too thin, and she was always trying to fatten me up.

1. fatten (someone) up
2. swear (someone) to secrecy
3. cloak of darkness
4. touch and go
5. waste away
6. head out
7. well done

Word Forms

Fill in the correct word form from those listed. Each form should be used.

1. decide, deciding, decision, decisive

   a. Returning Sam was a _____ moment in his life.

   b. His _____ turned out to be a good one.

   c. While Henry was _____ what to feed him, Sam ate the herring.

   d. Will you please _____ what you want to do?

2. waste, wasting, wasteful

   a. It is _____ to buy expensive fish food.

   b. Don't _____ your time talking to him.

   c. You're _____ your time looking for fish in this lake.

3. discover, discovering, discovery

   a. Henry made the _____ that Sam was a glutton.

   b. Henry was afraid that someone would _____ his plan.

   c. He was slowly _____ what Sam liked to eat.

4. refused, refusing, refusal

   a. Her _____ to go fishing annoyed him greatly.

   b. Sam _____ to eat and began wasting away.

   c. Henry was angry with Sam because he was _____ to cooperate.

5. cooperate, cooperative, cooperating, cooperation

   a. In order to win the contest, he needed his wife's _____ .

   b. Please be sure to _____ with the judges.

   c. After several days, Sam became very _____ .

   d. Because Sam was _____ , Henry managed to fatten him up quickly.

S*TRUCTURE*

Adjectives and Adverbs

Exercise 1

Underline the correct word (adjective or adverb) in the parentheses.
HINT: *Most adverbs end in -ly.*

EXAMPLE: Sherlock wagged his tail (eager, <u>eagerly</u>).

I have a pet dog named Sherlock. He's a cocker spaniel with (1. great, greatly), (2. brooding, broodingly) eyes. Sherlock is a very (3. trusting, trustingly) dog. But because he wants to protect me, whenever strangers come to the door, he gives them a (4. baleful, balefully) look.

Sherlock can be too protective. Once my friend John hit me in the stomach. It was an accident, but Sherlock didn't understand this. He barked (5. sharp, sharply) and made a (6. prodigious, prodigiously) leap into the air. He knocked my friend down.

(7. Sudden, Suddenly), we had a (8. ludicrous, ludicrously) situation. My pet (9. obvious, obviously) did not like my best friend. Each time John came to visit, Sherlock barked at him.

In order to solve the problem, I asked John to bring Sherlock a bone. He brought a (10. large, largely) bone from the butcher, and Sherlock grabbed it (11. eager, eagerly). This (12. simple, simply) plan was a success. Sherlock (13. gradual, gradually) began to like John again. Now my best friend is no longer my pet's worst enemy.

Exercise 2

Write a story about a pet. The story can be based on an experience or can be made up. It can be humorous or serious. Use lots of adjectives (to describe the pet and other nouns) and adverbs (to describe the action). Adjectives and adverbs should help your story paint a clear picture for readers or listeners. Read your story to the class. Do your classmates get a clear picture of what you're describing?

Comparatives and Superlatives of Adjectives

To form the comparative of an adjective, you can usually follow this rule:

Add *-er* to the end of the adjective if it has only one syllable (a spelling change might be needed). (For example, the comparative of *fat* is *fatter: Sam is fatter than most salmon.*)

Use *more* before the adjective if it has two or more syllables. (For example, the comparative of *cooperative* is *more cooperative: Sam was more cooperative after Henry fed him.*)

If a two-syllable adjective ends in *y,* use *-er* and change the *y* to *i* (for example, the comparative of *funny* is *funnier*).

Never use both *more* and *-er* in the same comparison.

To form the superlative of an adjective, you can usually follow this rule:

Add *-est* to the end of the adjective if it has only one syllable (a spelling change might be needed). (For example, the superlative of *fat* is *fattest: Sam is the fattest fish in the tank.*)

Use *most* before the adjective if it has two or more syllables. (For example, the superlative of *cooperative* is *most cooperative: Sam is the most cooperative pet that Henry ever had.*)

If a two-syllable adjective ends in y, use *-est* and change the *y* to *i* (for example, the superlative of *funny* is *funniest*).

Never use both *most* and *-est* in the same superlative.

Exercise 1

Fill in each blank with the correct form of the adjective in parentheses. Add -er, more, -est, *and* most *to get the correct form.*

EXAMPLE: Sam was the _____*smallest*_____ salmon he had
(small)
    ever caught.

1. If you want to eat the _____ fish, then you must
(fresh)
   catch it yourself.

2. Sam had the _____ eyes Henry had ever seen.
(baleful)

3. He was also the _____ fish he had ever seen.
(hungry)

4. Once Sam started eating, he actually seemed _____
(hungry)
   each day.

(Continued on next page)

5. Sam grew _____ by the day.
   (big)

6. After a few months, Sam needed a _____ tank
   (large)
   than he had before.

7. Henry hoped that Sam would grow to be the _____
   (gigantic)
   fish in the contest.

8. Soon Henry seemed to have a _____ relationship
   (close)
   with the fish than with his wife.

9. Sam jumped _____ than Henry had expected.
   (high)

10. Once when he jumped, Sam fell into the sawdust bin, because it
    was the _____ thing to the tank.
    (close)

11. Sam was also the _____ fish Henry had seen,
    (swift)
    even in the close quarters of the tank.

12. At the end of the year, Sam was even _____
    (heavy)
    than Henry had expected.

13. Sam seemed to be much _____ in the ocean
    (happy)
    than in the tank.

Exercise 2

The story also contains two common idiomatic uses of *more. More than* + adjective or adverb means *very.* For example, *The fish proved more than cooperative with Henry's plan to force-feed him* means that Sam was very cooperative with Henry's plan. *More and more* + adjective, adverb, or noun means "increasingly." For example, *Henry began spending more and more time in the basement* means that the amount of time Henry was there kept increasing.

Can you write a sentence for each of these two uses of more?

1. *more than* + adjective: _____

2. *more and more* + adjective: _____

Pronouns and Reflexive Pronouns

Exercise 1

*Pronouns take the place of nouns. Sometimes, grammar requires
that a pronoun be used. Other times, pronouns just make sentences
sound better by making it possible to avoid repeating the same
nouns over and over.*

*In each paragraph, substitute pronouns for nouns that have already
been mentioned in that paragraph.*

EXAMPLE: Henry was looking into the tank, munching on an apple when
Henry dropped the core. The salmon took the core at a gulp.
**Henry was looking into the tank, munching on an apple
when he dropped the core. The salmon took it at a gulp.**

1. Henry Pludge had a foolproof plan to win the fishing derby. The
plan was ludicrously simple. Henry decided that Henry would catch a
salmon, keep the salmon alive in a tank in Henry's basement, fatten the
salmon up for a year, and walk away with the first prize.

2. Henry built a large steel tank in Henry's basement, swore Henry's
wife to secrecy, and went fishing.

3. It was only in the spring that Sam appeared unhappy, and the
sound of Sam leaping and slapping the surface kept the Pludges awake
many nights. Once, the Pludges had to go down and carry Sam back to the
tank from the sawdust bin where a prodigious leap had carried Sam.

Exercise 2

Reflexive pronouns are pronoun forms with *-self.* They are used instead
of object pronouns when the noun they refer to is also the subject of
the sentence. For example, *Henry put himself in the tank* would mean
Henry went in the tank, but *Henry put him in the tank* would mean
that someone other than Henry went in the tank.

In each sentence, choose the reflexive pronoun or the object pronoun.

EXAMPLE: The sound of _____*him*_____ leaping and slapping
(him/himself)
the surface kept the Pludges awake.

(Continued on next page)

1. He had taken to calling _____ "Sam."
   (it/itself)

2. Sometimes he caught _____ talking to
   (him/himself)
   _____.
   (it/itself)

3. Like a goldfish in a small bowl, Sam adapted _____
   (him/himself)
   to his close quarters.

4. When Sam took the bait, Henry would conk _____
   (him/himself)
   on the skull.

5. "The poor fish," Henry was thinking to _____.
   (him/himself)

6. "I have denied _____ a whole year of freedom."
   (him/himself)

7. "I have kept _____ locked in a basement."
   (him/himself)

8. Henry decided he had to let _____ go.
   (him/himself)

9. Sam began to swim in small circles. Gradually Henry lost sight
   of _____.
   (him/himself)

10. If Henry had killed Sam to win the fishing derby, he would have
    hated _____.
    (him/himself)

Cloze Exercise

Fill in the blanks with any appropriate word. Make sure to choose a word from the part of speech (adjective, adverb, noun, verb, etc.) that is appropriate for the blank. Some blanks have more than one possible answer.

EXAMPLE: On ____*the*____ weekend, there ____*are*____

many sports ____*on*____ television.

Sports are _____ popular in
(1)

_____ United States. _____ sports can
(2)   (3)

_____ played all _____ round, while
(4)   (5)

_____ are played _____ a particular
(6)   (7)

_____. For example, baseball _____
      (8)   (9)

usually   played   _____   the   summer,
                               (10)

_____ football is _____ played in
      (11)   (12)

_____ fall. On _____ other hand,
      (13)   (14)

_____ like bowling _____ gymnastics
      (15)   (16)

are _____ all year _____. Believe it
        (17)   (18)

_____ not, fishing _____ a year-round
      (19)   (20)

_____. In the _____, fishers can
      (21)   (22)

_____ holes in _____ ice and
      (23)   (24)

_____ in these _____.
      (25)   (26)

*F*OLLOW UP

Topics for Discussion

1. Why do people have pets?
2. What kind of pet would you most like to have? What kind of pet would you least like to have? Explain your answers.
3. What is the most unusual kind of pet you have ever heard of?
4. Some humor in this story comes from Sam's eating foods that people in North America often eat. If you were entertaining friends, and you wanted to introduce them to a new food, what would you serve them? Which foods do you like the best? Which do you like the least?
5. Do you like fish? To look at in an aquarium? To keep in your home as pets? To eat? To catch?

Topics for Writing

1. In a three-paragraph essay, describe a pet you had and what you liked and disliked about it.
2. Were you ever in a contest? If so, what contest was it and what happened?

(Continued on next page)

3. Pretend you're going to dine out. In a two-paragraph essay, describe your ideal restaurant and your favorite meal. (Don't worry about the cost.)

4. People who fish often like to brag about the huge fish they have caught or have almost caught. If you like to fish, tell a story about a big fish you caught or a big fish that got away.

5. Pretend that salmon can talk and that you are Sam. With a classmate, write a dialogue in which you tell another salmon, whom you've just met after being let go, about your year at Henry Pludge's house.

6. How did Henry manage to keep Sam a secret? With a classmate, write a dialogue in which a friend of Henry's comes over and wants to know why he's not allowed in the basement anymore. Henry has to try to make excuses to keep his friend out of the basement.

7. What would have happened if Henry had carried out his plan? Would he have won the fishing derby? Would his cheating have been discovered? Would he have felt guilty about killing Sam and/or about cheating? Write a different ending to the story, in which Henry goes through with his plan.

8. Are you a good loser? With some classmates, write a dialogue describing a situation where you did not win or get what you wanted. Be sure to describe what you did after losing.

Learn with BOOK

—R. J. HEATHORN

Learn with BOOK

◆ **PREVIEWING THE STORY**

*Look at the picture, the title, and the first paragraph of the
story. Answer the questions, explaining each answer.*

1. What do you think this story is about?

2. What is BOOK? How is it described in the first paragraph?

3. Based on the first paragraph, what is the author criticizing in
    this story?

4. How do you think this story will differ from other stories in
    this book?

◆ **THINKING ABOUT THE TOPIC**

Think about and answer the following questions.

1. Why does the author make BOOK sound like a new invention?

2. In addition to books, what are some of the other ways of
    presenting information? How do they compare with books?

3. In your home town, what role do audiovisual aids and computers
    play in the schools? Is their role increasing?

A new aid to rapid[1]—almost magical[2]—learning has made its appearance.* Indications[3] are that if it catches on,* all the electronic gadgets will be so much* junk.[4] The new device[5] is known as Built-in Orderly[6] Organized Knowledge. The makers generally call it by its initials, BOOK.

Many advantages are claimed over the old-style learning and teaching aids on which most people are brought up* nowadays. It has no wires, no electric circuits[7] to break down. No connection is needed to an electricity power plant. It is made entirely without mechanical parts to go wrong or need replacement.

Anyone can use BOOK, even children, and it fits comfortably into the hands. It can be conveniently used sitting in an armchair by the fire.

How does this revolutionary,[8] unbelievably easy invention[9] work? Basically BOOK consists only of a large number of paper sheets. These may run to hundreds where BOOK covers a lengthy program of information. Each sheet bears a number of sequence,[10] so that the sheets cannot be used in the wrong order. To make it even easier for the user to keep the sheets in the proper order they are held firmly in place by a special locking device called a "binding."

Each sheet of paper presents the user with an information sequence in the form of symbols[11] which he absorbs[12] optically[13] for automatic registration on the brain. When one sheet has been assimilated,[14] a mere flick[15] of the finger turns it over and further information is found on the other side. By using both sides of each sheet in this way, a great economy is effected,[16] thus reducing both the size and cost of BOOK. No buttons need to be pressed to move from one sheet to another, to open or close BOOK, or to start it working.

BOOK may be taken up at any time and used by merely opening it. Instantly it is ready to use. Nothing has to be connected up or switched[17] on. The user may turn at will* to any sheet, going backward or forward as he pleases. A sheet is provided near the beginning as a location finder for any required information sequence.

A small accessory,[18] available at trifling[19] extra cost, is the BOOKmark. This enables the user to pick up his program where he left

[1] fast
[2] having special powers
[3] signs
[4] worthless material
[5] tool
[6] neat

[7] paths of electrical currents

[8] very new and different
[9] new creation

[10] order in which things follow one another

[11] signs
[12] takes in
[13] with the eyes
[14] taken in, understood
[15] short, quick movement
[16] achieved; done

[17] turned

[18] something to use with something else
[19] very small; unimportant

115

[20] with many uses

[21] starting
[22] changes
[23] that can be thought of
[24] ability

[25] moving
[26] very clever
[27] registered to protect ownership rights

[28] disadvantages; problems

off on the previous learning session. BOOKmark is versatile[20] and may be used in any BOOK.

The initial[21] cost varies[22] with the size and subject matter. Already a vast range of BOOKS is available, covering every conceivable[23] subject and adjusted to different levels of aptitude.[24] One BOOK, small enough to be held in the hands, may contain an entire learning schedule. Once purchased, BOOK requires no further cost; no batteries or wires are needed, since the motive[25] power, thanks to the ingenious[26] device patented[27] by the makers, is supplied by the brain of the user.

BOOKS may be stored on handy shelves, and for ease of reference, the program schedule is normally indicated on the back of the binding.

Altogether the Built-in Orderly Organized Knowledge seems to have great advantages with no drawbacks.[28] We predict a great future for it. ◆

IDIOMS AND PHRASES*

make an appearance	*to be present*
to catch on	*become popular*
so much	*nothing but, as unimportant as*
to be brought up on	*to grow up with; to be educated with*
at will	*whenever (one) wants*

POST-READING

Comprehension

1. What do the initials BOOK stand for?

2. What is BOOK being compared to?

3. According to the author, what advantages does BOOK have over these "old-style" learning aids?

4. What are some of the features of BOOK that make it easy to use?

5. How is the author's description of BOOK similar to the description of a machine?

6. What accessory is there for BOOK, and how is this accessory used?

7. In the sentence, "Each sheet bears a number of sequence," what does "number of sequence" mean? What is the "location finder" that is provided near the beginning of a book? What is the "program schedule" indicated on the back of the binding?

Responding to the Story

1. Because we are all familiar with books, why does the author present BOOK as a new invention?

2. What argument is the author making through the story? Do you think this is a convincing way to make the argument?

3. How would you describe the writing in this story? How is it similar to the writing in instruction manuals you have read? What makes this story more interesting than an instruction manual?

VOCABULARY

Vocabulary Builder

Fill in each blank with the correct word in parentheses.

1. When a gadget is broken, it becomes _____.
   (junk, valuable)

2. If you want to make money from your _____,
   (sequence, invention)
   you must first have it _____.
   (patented, varied)

3. BOOK is not really a new _____ for learning.
   (gadget, indication)

4. Books can take you into a(n) _____ world.
   (effected, magical)

5. With books, you can _____ a lot of information.
   (absorb, flick)

6. Some people have an _____ for reading quickly
   (accessory, aptitude)
   and remembering what they read.

7. A person can make _____ progress in a
   (rapid, trifling)
   language by reading a great deal in that language.

8. At a library, you will find books on almost any

   _____ subject.
   (conceivable, versatile)

9. The only _____ to using the library is that you
   (drawback, symbol)
   have to return the books.

10. Even on a(n) _____ visit to the library, it's
    (versatile, initial)
    usually possible to borrow some books.

Idiom Exercise

Choose the idiom that is similar in meaning to the underlined word(s).

making an appearance   catching on
being brought up on   at will

1. Computer games are <u>becoming popular</u>.
2. Most children today are <u>growing up with</u> television.
3. She could recall the titles of the books she had read <u>whenever she wanted</u>.
4. He will be <u>present</u> at our book demonstration.

Word Forms

Exercise 1

Fill in the correct word form from those listed. Each form should be used.

1. magic, magical, magician
   a. The _____ pulled the book from his sleeve.
   b. Many fairy tales describe _____ worlds.
   c. After he read a book on _____, he knew how to do card tricks.

2. build, builder, building, built
   a. A book can help you _____ your vocabulary.
   b. The _____ who _____ this library did not realize how quickly our book collection would grow.
   c. We are planning to have a separate _____ to hold our magazine and newspaper collections.

3. teach, teacher, teaching
   a. Experience is the best _____.
   b. Will you _____ me how to remember what I read?
   c. _____ without books is very difficult.

4. comfort, comfortable, comforting

    a. When you read, do you sit in a _____ chair?

    b. Reading a good book on a rainy day is very _____.

    c. He is feeling sad because he lost his favorite book, so let's try
       to _____ him.

5. inform, informative, information

    a. Please _____ her if you're going to the library.

    b. Mr. Parker gave an _____ lecture on the benefits
       of reading.

    c. There is very little _____ about Africa in this book.

Exercise 2

*Change each word or word part in Column A into a new word by
adding to it an appropriate word or word part from Column B. Each
item in Column B should be used only once.*

A	B
1. access *ory* _____	back
2. arm _____	in
3. back _____	ally
4. basic _____	ary
5. book _____	~~ory~~
6. draw _____	al
7. electron _____	ing
8. entire _____	ic
9. _____ genious	adays
10. inform _____	ly
11. learn _____	chair
12. magic _____	ation
13. no _____	thing
14. now _____	mark
15. revolution _____	ward

$TRUCTURE

Subject–Verb Agreement

In a sentence, the subject and verb must agree in number. Underline the subject and circle the correct verb in each of the following sentences. Remember: The subject is usually at the beginning of the sentence. Treat only one word as the subject.

EXAMPLE: A new <u>aid</u> to learning ((has,) have) made its appearance.

1. Indications (is, are) that if it (catch, catches) on, all the electronic gadgets will be so much junk.

2. Many advantages (are, is) claimed over the old-style learning and teaching aids on which most people (is, are) brought up nowadays.

3. Each sheet (bear, bears) a number of sequence, so that the sheets cannot be used in the wrong order.

4. Each sheet of paper (present, presents) the user with an information sequence in the form of symbols, which he (absorb, absorbs) optically for automatic registration on the brain.

5. When one sheet (has, have) been assimilated, a mere flick of the finger (turns, turn) it over and further information (is, are) found on the other side.

6. By using both sides of each sheet in this way, a great economy (is, are) effected.

7. No buttons (need, needs) to be pressed to move from one sheet to another.

8. Nothing (has, have) to be connected up or switched on.

9. The user may turn at will to any sheet, going backward or forward as he (please, pleases).

10. A small accessory, available at trifling extra cost, (is, are) the bookmark.

11. The motive power, thanks to the ingenious device patented by the makers, (is, are) supplied by the brain of the user.

Active and Passive Sentences

A sentence with an object often can be expressed not only as an active sentence but also as a passive sentence. In an active sentence, the subject of the sentence does the action. In a passive sentence, the subject receives the action. Compare the following active and passive sentences:

Many people use BOOK. (Active)

BOOK is used by many people. (Passive)

(In these sentences, people do the action of reading, and the book "receives" this action.)

To change an active sentence into a passive sentence, you must:

1. put the object of the active sentence into subject position;

2. add a form of *be* (the form that agrees with the subject of the passive sentence and that is in the same tense) and follow it with the past participle form of the verb in the sentence (*used* is the past participle of *use*);

3. add *by* + the subject of the active sentence to the end of the passive sentence.

If the subject of the active sentence is not important, it can be left out of the passive sentence. For example, the passive sentence corresponding to *People often read books more than once* can be expressed as *Books are often read more than once; by people* is not needed.

Change the following active sentences to passive sentences. Use by + *active subject only if indicated.*

EXAMPLES: People know the device as BOOK.
The device is known as BOOK.

Each sheet of paper can present an information sequence. (by)
An information sequence can be presented by each sheet of paper.

1. Anyone can use BOOK. (by)

2. People claim many advantages.

3. People can use it conveniently.

4. People effect a great economy.

5. We predict a great future for it.

6. The user absorbs the information. (by)

7. The makers patented the ingenious device. (by)

8. Each sheet presents an information sequence. (by)

9. A special locking device holds the sheets. (by)

10. People may use BOOKmark in any book.

11. BOOK will replace electronic gadgets. (by)

Phrasal Verbs

Exercise 1

Phrasal verbs, or two-word verbs, consist of a verb followed by a preposition or adverb. For example, *look into*, meaning "investigate," *put out*, meaning "extinguish," and *run into*, meaning "accidentally meet," are phrasal verbs.

Complete each sentence with a phrasal verb from the list below. Change the form of the verb if necessary. Use each verb only once.

EXAMPLE: When you want to use BOOK, there is nothing that has to be _____*connected up.*_____

break down	catch on	connect up	leave off
pick up	switch on	turn over	turn to

1. Not only is there nothing that has to be _____, but there are no electric circuits to _____, so repairs are never needed.
2. Unlike old-style learning aids, BOOK doesn't have to be _____ in order to be used.
3. The user can _____ any sheet in BOOK, going backward or forward as he pleases.
4. With a BOOKmark, the user can easily _____ in the place where he _____ the last time he used BOOK. (two phrasal verbs)
5. If BOOK _____, nobody will use electronic gadgets anymore.

Exercise 2

Like regular verbs, some phrasal verbs take objects and others do not. For example, *get in* does not take an object *(We got in late last night)*, but *run into* does *(We ran into Bob last night)*. A phrasal verb that takes an object can be inseparable or separable. If a phrasal verb is inseparable, the object must follow both its words; for example, *Bob* must come after *ran into*. If a phrasal verb is separable, the object can come between the two words. Pronoun objects must come between the two words. For example, *call up* is a separable phrasal verb, and the following three sentences are all possible:

I called up Bob.
I called Bob up.
I called him up.

Phrasal verbs are often used in conversation. With a classmate, write a dialogue in which you include at least eight phrasal verbs from the following list. (If you are not sure of the meaning of some of the words, check in a dictionary.) You can base the dialogue on a scene from a book you have read (or from a movie you have seen) or on anything else you want. When you are satisfied with your dialogue, act it out for the class.

call up	drop in	figure out	get along (with)
get back (from)	get on	get out	get through
give back	give up	leave out	look up
make up	pay back	pick up	put back
put down	put off	put together	run into
run out (of)	think up	throw out	try on
try out	turn down	turn up	wake up
watch out (for)	write down		

Follow Up

Topics for Discussion

1. Like computers, television often takes the place of books. How would you convince someone who watches a lot of television to do some reading for pleasure instead?

2. There are many different types of reading, or uses for reading—for example, studying, reading for pleasure, reading to get specific information, etc. Think about this past week. What were some of the types of reading that you did?

3. When you read for pleasure, what type(s) of books do you like best—poetry, biography, mystery, adventure, romance, or something else? Why?

4. According to the story, books can be read anywhere. But in reality people usually read better under some conditions than under others. What conditions make it hard for you to read (noise, an uncomfortable chair, etc.)? What conditions make it easy for you to read?

5. The story tells about the advantages of books over computers and other electronic ways of presenting information. What are some of the advantages of electronic ways of presenting information?

(Continued on next page)

6. Suppose that at some future time, books no longer exist, and all information is presented electronically. What would this be like? Would people who had been brought up on books miss books? Would the absence of books be a serious loss or would electronic forms of presenting information work just as well?

Topics for Writing

1. Write a paragraph describing books without comparing them to a machine as the story does.

2. Your friend has asked you for a good book to read. Write a paragraph about a book you liked and why you liked it. Be sure to include the author and title of the book.

3. Write a paragraph telling about the advantages of reading.

4. Pretend that you have traveled into the future and come back to our time. Write two paragraphs describing what the future is like: What new things are there? What things from today no longer exist?

5. Write a paragraph in which you describe something familiar as if it were an exciting new invention. Make your description detailed like the description in the story.

The Miracle Drugs* Abroad

— ART BUCHWALD

The Miracle Drugs* Abroad

♦ **PREVIEWING THE STORY**

Look at the picture, the title, and the first paragraph of the story. Answer the questions, explaining each answer.

1. What is a "miracle drug"?

2. What do you think the story might be about?

3. What is a hypochondriac?

♦ **THINKING ABOUT THE TOPIC**

Think about and answer the following questions.

1. What are some common problems that people take pills for?

2. What are some of the "miracle drugs" that are available?

3. Think of a country other than the United States. How can you get medicine there?

4. In addition to a doctor, whom would you ask for medical advice?

5. What are some possible problems with taking pills?

S ome time ago the American boss of a friend of mine told the friend, "I admire you people who live abroad.[1] You don't take pills. In America we're always taking a pill for something or other. We're becoming a nation of hypochondriacs.[2] But you people here don't depend on pills."

My friend agreed. "We can't get any."

Well, it was a good story, but not necessarily true. The majority of Americans coming to Europe are weighted down with* every imaginable medication[3] prescribed[4] by family doctors. Each one is a miracle drug in its own right,* and I haven't met an American tourist yet who isn't willing to share his medicines with the less fortunate people who live abroad.

Just recently I had the occasion to see how many Americans will come to the aid of* their fellow men. It all started off when I complained at a dinner party of having a sore throat.

"I have just the thing* for you," the hostess said. "It's Slipawhizdrene. You take one every two hours."

One of the guests said, "Slipawhizdrene is outdated.[5] My doctor gave me Heventizeall. It doesn't make you as sleepy, and you only have to take two every four hours."

"I left the United States two weeks after you did," another woman said, "and Heventizeall has been superseded[6] by Deviltizeall. I have a bottle at the hotel, and if you stop by* I'll give you some."

The only Frenchman at the table said, "Why don't you gargle[7] with aspirin?"

The people at the dinner couldn't have been more shocked if he had said a four-letter word.* The Frenchman's American wife was so embarrassed she almost broke into tears.*

He looked around helplessly. "But what did I say wrong?"

The husband of the hostess tried to smooth things over.* "You see, René, in America we have gone beyond aspirin. You French believe in food; we believe in miracle drugs."

"They're all barbarians,"[8] muttered[9] one of the Americans.

After dinner I stopped by the hotel and picked up an envelope of Deviltizeall. I took two before I went to bed. At four in the morning I no

---

[1] in a foreign country

[2] people who always think they're ill

[3] drug
[4] ordered

[5] old; no longer much used

[6] replaced

[7] rinse the throat

[8] rough, uncivilized people
[9] said in a low voice

[10] extremely; painfully

[11] person in control of making a movie

longer had my sore throat, but I was violently[10] sick to my stomach.* I had a luncheon date with a Hollywood producer,[11] but I couldn't eat anything.

"I've got just the thing for an upset stomach. It's called Egazzakine. Here, take one now, and one at four o'clock."

[12] offered

[13] become watery

I took the proffered[12] pill, and in a half-hour my stomach settled. Only now, my eyes started to run,[13] and I began sneezing.

[14] signs of illness

[15] sensitivity to something eaten, taken, or breathed

Making my way blindly to the office, I ran into another American friend in front of the Lancaster Hotel. He recognized the symptoms[14] immediately. "You've probably got an allergy.[15] Come upstairs and I'll give you something for it."

We went up to his room, and he took out a leather case filled with various bottles.

[16] liver illness

[17] infection of the lungs

[18] pain in the joints or muscles

"Let's see," he said, reading from a slip of paper. "The yellow-and-black ones are for jaundice,[16] the green-and-blue ones are for pneumonia,[17] the white-and-red ones are for rheumatism,[18] the pink-and-beige ones are for heart trouble—oh, yes, the brown-and-purple are for allergies. Here, take two now, and two at four o'clock."

"But," I protested, "I've got to take the Egazzakine at four o'clock."

"Don't do it," he warned. "That's what you're probably allergic to."

[19] medicine in a small container that can be swallowed

[20] passages

I took the brown-and-purple capsules[19] and went to the office. In about an hour, my tear ducts[20] had dried up and I had stopped sneezing.

I felt perfectly well, except that I couldn't move my left arm.

I reported this to my friend at the Lancaster, who said, "The doctor warned me it happens sometimes. He gave me something else in case it did. I'll send it over with the bellboy."[21]

[21] hotel worker

[22] cherry color

[23] pills

The bellboy brought over some orange-and-cerise[22] tablets.[23]

I took two, and it wasn't long before I could lift my arm again.

That evening during dinner I discovered I had my sore throat back. But I didn't mention it to a soul.* ◆

IDIOMS AND PHRASES*

miracle drugs	*drugs that are new and work very well*
be weighted down with	*be loaded with; have a lot of*
in its own right	*by itself*
come to the aid of	*help*
just the thing	*the perfect thing*
to stop by	*to make a short visit*

four-letter word	*a "bad" or "dirty" word (in English, these*
	words often have four letters)
broke into tears	*started crying*
to smooth things over	*to make something more pleasant*
sick to my stomach	*feeling very bad in the stomach*
not . . . to a soul	*not to anyone*

POST-READING

Comprehension

1. What was the narrator's original illness?

2. To whom did he complain about his illness?

3. What did the Americans say? What did the Frenchman say?

4. Why were the Americans shocked by the Frenchman's suggestion?

5. What happened after the narrator took Deviltizeall?

6. What happened after he took Egazzakine?

7. What happened after he took the brown-and-purple capsules? After he took the orange-and-cerise tablets?

8. Were all the drugs he tried good for curing a sore throat? Why did he have to cure other illnesses?

9. At the end of the story, why didn't the narrator want to tell anyone that his throat hurt?

Responding to the Story

1. At the beginning of the story and at the end of the story, the narrator is in the same situation—he's at a dinner party, and he has a sore throat. Why is this funny?

2. What does the author's attitude toward miracle drugs seem to be?

3. Why does the author include the conversation about Slipawhizdrene, Heventizeall, and Deviltizeall? What specifically is he making fun of with this conversation? What are fads? What other fads can you think of?

4. Why do the made-up names of drugs and the listing of the colors of capsules help to make the story funny?

5. If, like the narrator, you had a sore throat, what would you do? Would you take medicine? If so, what medicine would you take? If not, what would you do instead?

VOCABULARY

Vocabulary Builder

Exercise 1

Say whether you agree or disagree with each of the following statements. Give reasons for your answers.

1. If you live <u>abroad</u>, you might have to take a plane home for the holidays.
2. If you are a <u>hypochondriac</u>, you are always sick.
3. Only teachers can <u>prescribe</u> <u>medication</u>.
4. When you choose a doctor, you want to make sure that his treatments are <u>outdated</u>.
5. When someone is very polite, he behaves like a <u>barbarian</u>.
6. Someone who is <u>violently</u> sick is behaving in an angry way because of illness.
7. Feeling strong is a <u>symptom</u> of illness.
8. If you have <u>rheumatism</u>, your eyes hurt.
9. If you have <u>pneumonia</u>, you have an infection of the lungs.
10. If you have an <u>allergy</u>, you never cough or sneeze.
11. Hand packaging of medication has been <u>superseded</u> by machine packaging.
12. Many patients refuse the <u>proffered</u> medicine even though it will make them feel better.

Exercise 2

ROLE PLAY: Pretend you are a patient going to visit a doctor because you don't feel well. What questions would the doctor ask you? What questions would you ask him or her? With a partner, write a dialogue between a doctor and a patient and act it out for the class. Use some of the following vocabulary words and other related words from the story.

allergy/allergic	gargle
medication	miracle drug
prescribe	sick to (one's) stomach
symptom	

Idiom Exercise

Fill in each blank with the appropriate idiom from the list.

weighted down with	broke into tears
came to her aid	sick to my stomach
stop by	to smooth things over

The medical student was _____ books, so he
(1)
decided to rest on a park bench. He sat down next to a woman and

smiled at her. But as he did, she _____ . "What's the
(2)
matter?" he asked. He was worried that somehow he had offended

her, and he wanted _____.
(3)

"Oh, I don't know," she replied. "Suddenly I feel completely

_____."
(4)

The student could see that she looked really sick. "You'd better go

to the hospital," he said. "I'll call an ambulance."

He ran to call the ambulance for the woman, and within minutes it

_____.
(5)

As she was helped into the ambulance, the student said, "Don't

worry. It's a good hospital. I'm in training there, and if you need to

stay over, I'll _____ to see you tomorrow if you want."
(6)

Thus, the young medical student practiced the first lesson of

medical school—do not treat a patient until you are a doctor.

Say It Right

How many of these words can you pronounce correctly?
Try them and see.

1. hypochondriac   Hai poh KAHN dree ak
2. miracle   MIR uh kl
3. prescribed   pri SKRAIBD
4. violently   VAI uh lent lee

(Continued on next page)

5. proffered   PRAH ferd
6. allergy   A ler jee
7. jaundice   JAWN dis
8. pneumonia   nuh MOH nyuh
9. rheumatism   ROO muh ti zuhm
10. embarrassed   em BER res d

Prefixes and Suffixes

A prefix is a word part that is added to the beginning of a word. When a prefix is used, it changes the meaning of the word. For example, *un-* changes *important* to its opposite, *unimportant.*

A suffix is a word part that is added to the end of a word. When a suffix is used, it often changes the word's grammatical function. For example, the suffix *-or* changes the verb *act* to the noun *actor.*

Exercise 1

Prefixes have particular meanings. If you know the meaning of a prefix and of the word it is added to, you can often figure out the meaning of the new word. Some common prefixes and their meanings are:

> *un*—not; the opposite
> *ab*—away from
> *pre*—before in time or place
> *super*—above; more than
> *anti*—against
> *post*—after
> *dis*—away; apart

Tell whether each sentence is true or false. Your answers will be based on the meaning of the prefix in the underlined words. In your own words, explain the meaning of each underlined word. You may use a dictionary to help you.

1. If the doctor prescribes <u>postoperative</u> bed rest, the patient should take plenty of time to rest before his operation.
2. If a person makes a <u>superhuman</u> effort, the effort wasn't easy for him.
3. If a person has a <u>dislocated</u> shoulder, the bone is pulled away from where it should be.
4. Falling asleep is an <u>abnormal</u> effect of taking a sleeping pill.
5. If a person is feeling depressed and unhappy for a period of time, his doctor might prescribe an <u>antidepressant</u>.

6. If a person's headaches <u>predated</u> her illness, the illness probably isn't causing the headaches.

7. If a doctor is <u>uncertain</u> about what a patient's symptoms mean, the doctor will not need to further examine the patient.

Exercise 2

Some suffixes make words into nouns. These suffixes include *-er, -or, -ion, -ment, -ness, -ant, -ist, -an,* and *-ence.* Can you think of nouns with some of these suffixes?

Suffixes that make words into verbs include *-ize, -fy, -ate,* and *-en.* Can you think of verbs with some of these suffixes?

Suffixes that make words into adjectives include *-ful, -al, -able, -ible, -ive, -ed* (which is also used for the past tense of verbs), and *-ing* (which also has other uses). Adverbs are often formed from the suffix *-ly.*

For each sentence, circle the letter of all the words that could be put in the blank in the sentence. An important clue will be the suffix (in bold type). Even if a word is unfamiliar, the suffix should help you decide whether the word fits into the sentence. There are several correct words for each sentence.

1. Some American travelers are weighted down with every imaginable _____.
   a. conveni**ence**
   b. conveni**ent**
   c. medic**ation**
   d. medic**ate**
   e. amuse**ment**
   f. amus**ing**
   g. possess**ion**
   h. possess**ive**

2. Mr. Smith invited his _____ to dinner.
   a. doctor**al**
   b. dent**ist**
   c. account**ant**
   d. employ**er**
   e. doctor
   f. dent**al**
   g. account**able**
   h. employ**ing**

3. The employees went in early to _____ the doctor's office.
   a. straight**en**
   b. straight**ness**
   c. decor**ate**
   d. decor**ative**
   e. beauti**fy**
   f. beauti**ful**
   g. steril**ize**
   h. sterile

4. Jane and John have a new friend who is a(n) _____.
   a. profess**or**
   b. profess
   c. art**ist**
   h. artful**ly**
   e. psycholog**ist**
   f. psycholog**ical**
   g. programm**er**
   i. programm**ing**

Understanding Drug Labels

Medicines can be very helpful. They can relieve symptoms and reduce pain. However, they can be harmful, too. Therefore, it is very important to read drug labels carefully because they contain the information you need in order to use the medicine correctly.

Exercise 1: Vocabulary Review

These are words that you should know in order to read and understand labels. In the following sentences fill in each blank with a word from the list, making the words plural if necessary. You may use your dictionary to help you.

prescription	symptom
side effect	dose
warning	refill

1. The _____ from some medicines may be headaches or sleepiness.
2. One _____ of a cold is a sore throat.
3. Only a doctor can write a _____.
4. A _____ on the label tells you of the possible dangers of the drug.
5. Some drug labels suggest different _____ for people of different ages.
6. If the drugstore label indicates a _____, the patient can get more of a prescription medicine without calling his or her doctor.

Exercise 2: Prescription Drugs

Below is a label from a prescription drug—a drug that can only be obtained at the request of a doctor. Read the label and answer the questions that follow.

ARNIE'S DRUGS
25600 Frankel Street
Tulsa, Oklahoma
Phone: NE8-5000
Reg. No. 3255   RX#1234

Patient Anna Fields
Address 52 Pine   No Refills
One teaspoon four (4) times a day
Dr. Pillsbury   Reg. No. 5689
Address 86 Olive   Date 2/11/19___

Fill in the blanks with the correct information from the label.

1. _____ is the only person who should take this medicine.

2. _____ should be taken for each dose.

3. A total of _____ teaspoons should be taken in a day.

4. The person who prescribed this medicine is _____.

5. The patient can have this prescription refilled _____

Exercise 3: Over-the-Counter Medicine

Below is a label from an over-the-counter drug—a drug you can buy without a prescription. Read the label and answer the questions that follow.

No-Cold

CHERRY LOZENGES
anesthetic-antiseptic

For fast temporary relief of minor sore-throat pain.

USE ACCORDING TO DIRECTIONS:

ADULTS: Dissolve 1 lozenge every 2 hours. Do not exceed 8 per day.
Children 6 to 12: Dissolve 1 lozenge every 3 hours. Do not exceed 4 per day.
Active ingredients: Phenol, sodium phenolate (total phenol 32.5 mg). Avoid excessive heat (over 104°F or 40°C).

WARNING: Consult physician if sore throat is severe or lasts more than 2 days or is accompanied by high fever, headache, nausea, or vomiting. Not for children under 6 unless directed by physician.

KEEP ALL MEDICINES OUT OF REACH OF CHILDREN.
Made in U.S.A. by National Pharmaceuticals, Inc.
Distributed by Mabro Corp.

Cincinnati, Ohio 45202431101–1

---

1. What is the name of this product?

2. What symptoms is this product supposed to relieve?

3. How much of this product is to be taken for each dose?

4. How often may a dose be taken?

5. What is the maximum amount of this product that can be taken in a twenty-four-hour period?

6. What signals mean that you should stop using this product?

7. About what else should the user be careful?

To Make

Make *is an overused word. Below are sentences which can be improved by substituting another word for* make. *Read each sentence. Think of a more exact word to use instead of* make *and write it over the word* make. *Do not use any word more than once. Do not change other words.*

          Prepare
EXAMPLE: ~~Make~~ a solution of vinegar and water to put on
               your sunburn.

1. The doctor asked the child to make a picture of where it hurt him.
2. Many drug companies make aspirin.
3. The builder decided to make both buildings of the hospital alike.
4. If you feel cold, ask someone to make you a scarf.
5. I'm going to make a cake for my friend who is sick in the hospital.
6. If Mark continues studying, he will make a good doctor.
7. John takes that make of vitamins because they contain a lot of calcium.
8. Let's make another appointment for your examination.
9. When you add fifty dollars to your medical expenses, it will make two hundred dollars that you have already spent.
10. Some doctors make a good deal of money.
11. Dr. Jones bought a large apartment, which he will make into three examination rooms.
12. The author will make a short speech at the dinner party.
13. We should make the date for taking our blood tests.
14. I will make chicken soup for my sister who has a cold.

STRUCTURE

Cloze Exercise

Fill in the blanks with any appropriate word.

Some time ago _____ (1) American boss of _____ (2) friend of mine _____ (3) my friend, "I _____ (4) you people who _____ (5) abroad. You don't _____ (6) pills. In America we're _____ (7) taking a pill _____ (8) something or other. _____ (9) becoming a nation _____ (10) hypochondriacs. But you people here _____ (11) depend on pills."

The Pronoun *It*

It can refer to a specific thing or to something more abstract like a thought or idea that has been expressed. Sometimes, *it* doesn't refer to anything but just fills a place in the sentence, as in *It is raining* or *It was five o'clock when Susan arrived.*

Find each sentence in the story, and, by looking back at the sentences before it, decide what the pronoun it *is referring to. In one sentence it* doesn't refer to anything. *Can you figure out which sentence that is?*

EXAMPLE: Well, *it* was a good story, but not necessarily true.

> *It* refers to the friend's saying that people living in Europe can't get any pills.

1. *It* doesn't make you as sleepy, and you only have to take two every four hours.

   _____

2. *It's* called Egazzakine.

   _____

3. Come upstairs and I'll give you something for *it*.

   _____

(Continued on next page)

4. Don't do *it*.

_____

5. The doctor warned me *it* happens sometimes. He gave me something else in case it did.

_____

6. I'll send *it* over with the bellboy.

_____

7. *It* wasn't long before I could lift my arm again.

_____

8. But I didn't mention *it* to a soul.

_____

Direct and Indirect Objects

Some English sentences do not have objects but only have a subject (e.g., *I felt perfectly fine*). Other sentences have a subject and a direct object (e.g., *I ate dinner*). Still other sentences have a subject, a direct object, and an indirect object (e.g., *The hostess showed the bottle to her guests*). The direct object is the object that is being acted on (in this case, the bottle, which is being shown). The indirect object is the object to whom or for whom the action is being performed (in this case, her guests, to whom the bottle is being shown).

With many verbs, a sentence with an indirect object can be expressed in two ways:

    1. verb + direct object + *to/for* + indirect object
       I offered the car to Paul.
    2. verb + indirect object + direct object
       I offered Paul the car.

With some verbs (e.g., *explain, report, open*) only the first type of sentence is possible.

Exercise 1

Some of the following sentences have only a direct object; others have a direct object and an indirect object. In each sentence, underline the noun or pronoun that is the direct object and, if there is an indirect object, circle the noun or pronoun that is the indirect object.

EXAMPLE: The hostess offered (me) some <u>coffee</u> with my dessert.

1. You don't take pills.
2. I have just the thing for you.
3. Heventizeall doesn't make you sleepy.
4. I have a bottle at the hotel.

5. I'll give you some pills.

6. I no longer had my sore throat.

7. I couldn't eat the food.

8. I ran into an American friend.

9. He recognized the symptoms.

10. I reported this to my friend.

11. The doctor gave me something.

12. I'll send it to you.

13. I didn't mention it to a soul.

Exercise 2

Rewrite the sentences (if possible) by changing the position of the indirect object. You may add or remove the preposition to *as needed. Some sentences cannot be rewritten.*

1. I'll give some to you.

2. I reported this to my friend at the Lancaster.

3. The doctor gave me something.

4. I didn't mention it to a soul.

5. I'll send it to you.

6. I have just the thing for you.

7. I'll give you the medicine.

8. He offered me them.

FOLLOW UP

Topics for Discussion

1. Did you ever take a drug that made you feel sick? What happened?

2. The narrator is taking drugs that have been prescribed for other people. Why is this not a good idea?

3. The narrator feels worse when he tries to follow his friends' advice. What about you? What kinds of advice have your friends given you when you've been sick? Was this advice helpful? Explain.

(Continued on next page)

4. When you are ill, do you want to be left alone or do you want company and/or help? Explain.

5. What common medicines have you used that you think work especially well?

6. The Frenchman mentions an old cure for sore throats—a cure that does not involve miracle drugs. What are some cures you know of for sore throats or other common problems that don't involve drugs?

7. People are often especially afraid of becoming ill while traveling. Why is that? Have you ever gotten sick while traveling? What happened?

Topics for Writing

1. Write a paragraph describing your last illness. In your description, include the symptoms you had and the medicines you took.

2. In two paragraphs, compare the medical care you received in one city or country with the medical care you received in another city or country.

3. Look at the labels of four medicines you have in your house. List the names of the medicines and the possible side effects that are mentioned on the labels.

4. Did you ever have a friend who was a hypochondriac? In two paragraphs, describe this friend. How did you and other people react to his or her complaints? What happened to your friend? Did he or she become less of a hypochondriac?

5. This story is partly about a cultural difference between French people and Americans—a difference in attitudes toward medicine. Write two paragraphs about a cultural difference between Americans and people in another country.

6. In this story, whenever the narrator tries to fix one problem, another problem results. Write a short story in which a person's attempts to fix a problem lead to other problems. What happens in the end? Are the problems solved? Your story can be humorous or serious.

My Father Goes to Court

—C_ARLOS_ B_ULOSAN_

My Father Goes to Court

◆ **PREVIEWING THE STORY**

Look at the picture, the title, and the first paragraph of the story. Answer the questions, explaining each answer.

1. In what country does this story take place?

2. Where are the people in the picture? Can you guess who any of them are?

3. What seems to be happening in the picture?

◆ **THINKING ABOUT THE TOPIC**

Think about and answer the following questions.

1. What are the benefits of laughter?

2. How important is money to family happiness? Are families with money more likely to be happy than families without money?

3. Why might it be more difficult to go to court and win a case against a rich man?

When I was four, I lived with my mother and brothers and sisters in a small town on the island of Luzon. Father's farm had been destroyed in 1918 by one of our sudden Philippine floods, so for several[1] years afterward we all lived in the town, though he preferred living in the country. We had as a next door neighbor a very rich man, whose sons and daughters seldom came out of the house. While we boys and girls played and sang in the sun, his children stayed inside and kept the windows closed. His house was so tall that his children could look in the windows of our house and watch us as we played, or slept, or ate, when there was any food in the house *to* eat.

Now, this rich man's servants were always frying and cooking something good, and the aroma[2] of the food was wafted[3] down to us from the windows of the big house. We hung about[*] and took all the wonderful smell of the food into our beings. Sometimes, in the morning, our whole family stood outside the windows of the rich man's house and listened to the musical sizzling[4] of thick strips of bacon or ham. I can remember one afternoon when our neighbor's servants roasted three chickens. The chickens were young and tender and the fat that dripped into the burning coals gave off an enchanting[5] odor.[6] We watched the servants turn the beautiful birds and inhaled[7] the heavenly spirit that drifted out to us.

Some days the rich man appeared at a window and glowered[8] down at us. He looked at us one by one, as though he were condemning[9] us. We were all healthy because we went out in the sun every day and bathed in the cool water of the river that flowed from the mountains into the sea. Sometimes we wrestled[10] with one another in the house before we went out to play. We were always in the best of spirits[11] and our laughter was contagious.[12] Other neighbors who passed by our house often stopped in our yard and joined us in laughter.

Laughter was our only wealth. Father was a laughing man. He would go into the living room and stand in front of the tall mirror, stretching his mouth into grotesque[13] shapes with his fingers and making faces at himself; then he would rush into the kitchen, roaring with laughter.

There was always plenty to make us laugh. There was, for instance, the day one of my brothers came home with a small bundle under his arm, pretending that he brought something good to eat, maybe a leg of

[1] a few

[2] smell

[3] drifted

[4] noisy frying

[5] delightful

[6] smell

[7] breathed in

[8] looked angrily

[9] expressing strong disapproval

[10] fought playfully

[11] moods

[12] catching

[13] unusually odd

[14] too expensive

[15] untie

fist

[16] real; not pretended

[17] weak

[18] strong and healthy

[19] large group

[20] large sea animals

[21] strongest

[22] without cost

[23] life force

lamb or something as extravagant[14] as that, to make our mouths water.* He rushed to Mother and threw the bundle into her lap. We all stood around, watching Mother undo[15] the complicated strings. Suddenly a black cat leaped out of the bundle and ran wildly around the house. Mother chased my brother and beat him with her little fists,° while the rest of us bent double, choking with laughter.

We made so much noise that all our neighbors except the rich family came into the yard and joined us in loud, genuine[16] laughter.

It was like that for years.

As time went on, the rich man's children became thin and anemic,[17] while we grew even more robust[18] and full of life. Our faces were bright and rosy, but theirs were pale and sad. The rich man started to cough at night; then he coughed day and night. His wife began coughing too. The children started to cough, one after the other. At night their coughing sounded like the barking of a herd[19] of seals.[20] We hung outside their windows and listened to them. We wondered what had happened. We knew that they were not sick from lack of nourishing food, because they were still always frying something delicious to eat.

One day the rich man appeared at a window and stood there a long time. He looked at my sisters, who had grown fat with laughing, then at my brothers, whose arms and legs were like the *molave,* which is the sturdiest[21] tree in the Philippines. He banged down the window and ran through his house, shutting all the windows.

From that day on, the windows of our neighbor's house were always closed. The children did not come outdoors any more. We could still hear the servants cooking in the kitchen, and no matter how tight the windows were shut, the aroma of the food came to us in the wind and drifted gratuitously[22] into our house.

One morning a policeman from the *presidencia* came to our house with a sealed paper. The rich man had filed a complaint* against us. Father took me with him when he went to the town clerk and asked him what it was about. He told Father the man claimed that for years we had been stealing the spirit[23] of his wealth and food.

When the day came for us to appear in court, Father brushed his old Army uniform and borrowed a pair of shoes from one of my brothers. We were the first to arrive. Father sat on a chair in the center of the courtroom. Mother occupied a chair by the door. We children sat on a long bench by the wall. Father kept jumping up from his chair and stabbing the air with his arms, as though he were defending himself before an imaginary jury.[24]

The rich man arrived. He had grown old and feeble;[25] his face was scarred with deep lines. With him was his young lawyer. Spectators[26] came in and almost filled the chairs. The judge entered the room and sat on a high chair. We stood up in a hurry and then sat down again.

After the courtroom preliminaries,[27] the judge looked at Father. "Do you have a lawyer?" he asked.

"I don't need any lawyer, Judge," he said.

"Proceed,"[28] said the judge.

The rich man's lawyer jumped up and pointed his finger at Father. "Do you or do you not agree that you have been stealing the spirit of the complainant's wealth and food?"

"I do not!" Father said.

"Do you or do you not agree that while the complainant's servants cooked and fried fat legs of lamb or young chicken breasts you and your family hung outside his windows and inhaled the heavenly spirit of the food?"

"I agree," Father said.

"Do you or do you not agree that while the complainant and his children grew sickly and tubercular[29] you and your family became strong of limb* and fair of complexion?"[30]

"I agree," Father said.

"How do you account for that?"

Father got up and paced around, scratching his head thoughtfully. Then he said, "I would like to see the children of the complainant, Judge."

"Bring in the children of the complainant."

They came in shyly. The spectators covered their mouths with their hands, they were so amazed to see the children so thin and pale. The children walked silently to a bench and sat down without looking up. They stared at the floor and moved their hands uneasily.

Father could not say anything at first. He just stood by his chair and looked at them. Finally he said, "I should like to cross-examine[31] the complainant."

"Proceed."

"Do you claim that we stole the spirit of your wealth and became a laughing family while yours became morose[32] and sad?" Father asked.

---

[24] people who make decisions in court

[25] weak

[26] people who are watching

[27] introductory part

[28] begin; continue

[29] having a lung disease

[30] appearance of the skin

[31] ask questions of

[32] gloomy; bad-tempered

"Yes."

"Do you claim that we *stole* the spirit of your food by hanging outside your windows when your servants cooked it?" Father asked.

"Yes."

"Then we are going to *pay* you right now," Father said. He walked over to where we children were sitting on the bench and took my straw hat off my lap and began filling it up with centavo pieces that he took out of his pockets. He went to Mother, who added a fistful of silver coins. My brothers threw in their small change.

"May I walk to the room across the hall and stay there for a few minutes, Judge?" Father asked.

"As you wish."

[33] walked with long steps

"Thank you," Father said. He strode[33] into the other room with the hat in his hands. It was almost full of coins. The doors of both rooms were wide open.

"Are you ready?" Father called.

"Proceed," the judge said.

The sweet tinkle of the coins carried beautifully into the courtroom. The spectators turned their faces toward the sound with wonder. Father came back and stood before the complainant.

"Did you hear it?" he asked.

"Hear what?" the man asked.

"The spirit of the money when I shook the hat?" he asked.

"Yes."

"Then you are paid," Father said.

The rich man opened his mouth to speak and fell to the floor without a sound. The lawyer rushed to his aid. The judge pounded his gavel.[34]

[34] small wooden hammer

[35] ended; removed

[36] walked proudly

"Case dismissed,"[35] he said.

Father strutted[36] around the courtroom. The judge even came down from his high chair to shake hands with him. "By the way,"* he whispered, "I had an uncle who died laughing."

"You like to hear my family laugh, Judge?" Father asked.

"Why not?"

"Did you hear that, children?" Father asked.

My sisters started it. The rest of us followed them and soon the spectators were laughing with us, holding their bellies and bending over the chairs. And the laughter of the judge was the loudest of all. ◆

IDIOMS AND PHRASES*

hung about	*stayed nearby without any particular purpose*
to make one's mouth water	*to seem very desirable (usually said about food)*
filed a complaint	*reported a wrong in writing*
strong of limb	*healthy*
by the way	*phrase used to introduce an additional thought*

POST-READING

Comprehension

1. When and where does this story take place?
2. Describe the narrator and his family. How did they become poor?
3. Who was their neighbor? Describe some of the differences between the narrator's family and the family next door.
4. Why did the narrator and his family like to hang around near the neighbor's house?
5. What were some of the things that made the father and the others in the family laugh?
6. As time passed, what happened to the children in the two families?
7. Why did the rich man take the narrator's father to court?
8. How did Father defend himself in court?
9. What did the judge decide?

Responding to the Story

1. Why was the rich man so bothered by the narrator's family?
2. Would things have been any different for the rich man and his family if the narrator and his family had not been around? Would they have been any happier?
3. Why weren't the rich man and his family able to do the sorts of things their poor neighbors did?
4. What do you think the rich man hoped to accomplish by taking his neighbor to court?

(Continued on next page)

5. How do you think the narrator's family would have been, had they been rich?

6. What do you think of the father's argument in court?

7. Without Father's help, how would the judge have dealt with the case?

8. What message is the author trying to express with this story? Do you agree with this message?

VOCABULARY

Vocabulary Builder

Exercise 1

Replace the underlined word(s) in each sentence with the proper synonym from the list. Not all words in the list will be used.

several	contagious	proceed
aroma	grotesque	spectators
wafted	undo	complexion
sizzling	herd	complainant
enchanting	gratuitously	strutted
glowered	spirit	gavel
condemning	sturdy	strode
wrestled	preliminaries	limbs

1. The judge banged his <u>small wooden hammer</u> for order in the court.

2. After winning the case, Father <u>walked proudly</u> out of the courtroom.

3. The rich man accused Father of stealing the <u>life force</u> from his food.

4. Even after he closed the window, the <u>smell</u> of the rich man's food <u>drifted down</u> <u>without cost</u> into our house.

5. The boys <u>fought playfully</u> with each other.

6. We watched Mother <u>untie</u> the package.

7. The <u>noisy frying</u> of the meat made our mouths water.

8. The boys' arms and legs were very <u>strong</u>.

9. Laughter is <u>catching</u>, so soon the <u>people who were watching</u> began to laugh.

10. Because they were always indoors, their <u>skin's appearance</u> was pale.

11. <u>A few</u> times the judge advised him to <u>continue</u> with his cross-examination.

12. The children were so noisy that they sounded like a <u>large group</u> of animals.
13. The judge found the case to be <u>unusually odd</u>.
14. The rich man <u>looked angrily</u> at Father when he came into the courtroom.

Exercise 2

Role Play: With a classmate, write a dialogue between Father and the rich man, in which each explains his side of the argument to the court. In your dialogue, include as many of the above vocabulary words as you can. Then role-play the dialogue for your classmates.

Idiom Exercise

Use each of the underlined idioms in another sentence.

EXAMPLE: He was <u>bent double</u> with laughter.
> **I was bent double with a stomachache.**

1. The smell of the roast chicken <u>made my mouth water</u>.
   _____ made _____ mouth water.

2. The rich man <u>filed a complaint</u> against Father.
   _____ filed a complaint _____ .

3. I am going to court with Father; <u>by the way</u>, he'll be wearing his old Army uniform.
   _____ ; by the way, _____ .

4. We <u>hung about</u> and watched the rich man's guests go into the house for dinner.
   _____ hung about _____ .

Antonyms

In the blanks, write the opposites of the following words. Use your dictionary to help you. For most words, there is more than one correct answer.

1. destroyed _____
2. tender _____
3. inhaled _____
4. extravagant _____
5. complicated _____

(Continued on next page)

6. robust _____

7. feeble _____

8. morose _____

9. several _____

10. genuine _____

STRUCTURE

Cloze Exercise

Fill in the blanks with any appropriate word.

Now, this rich man's _____ (1) were always frying and _____ (2) something good, and the _____ (3) of the food was _____ (4) down to us from _____ (5) windows of the big _____ (6). We hung about and _____ (7) all the wonderful smells _____ (8) the food into our beings. Sometimes, _____ (9) the morning _____ (10) whole family stood outside _____ (11) windows of the _____ (12) house and listened to _____ (13) musical sizzling of thick strips of _____ (14) or ham. _____ (15) can remember one afternoon _____ (16) our neighbor's servants roasted _____ (17) chickens. The chickens were _____ (18) and tender and the _____ (19) that dripped into the _____ (20) coals gave off an _____ (21) odor. _____ (22) watched the servants turn the beautiful birds _____ (23) inhaled the heavenly spirit _____ (24) drifted out to us.

Summarizing Ideas

When you write a summary of something you have read, you write a short version of it, stating its main ideas in sentences of your own. Details should not be included in a summary.

Read the following paragraphs several times. Then close your book and write a summary of what you have read. Copy these words and expressions into your notebook, and use them in your summary:

file a complaint
store owner
hearing
manager
small claims court
sales receipt

Father Goes to Small Claims Court

Last year, Father bought a new oven for the family. He paid $300 for it. When the oven was delivered, one of the burners was not working. Father went back to the store and complained to the manager. The manager said he would take care of it. One week passed by, but no one came to our house to fix the oven. Father then wrote a letter of complaint to the owner of the store. Another week went by, but no one came to fix the stove. Father became very upset and decided to sue in small claims court where he could go at night to argue his case. For $3.90, Father filed a complaint and was given a hearing date.

The court sent a notice to the owner of the store about the complaint and informed him that the date of the hearing was March 24.

On March 24, Father took his sales receipt and went to court to argue before the judge. The owner of the store was also there. When the judge heard Father's story, he told the store owner to take back the stove and give Father back his money. Now Father can go to another store and buy a new stove.

Irregular Verbs—Past Tense

Exercise 1

Fill in the blanks with the past tense of the verb in parentheses.

1. The rich man's children never laughed or _____.
   (sing)

2. They never even _____ out of their house.
   (come)

3. The rich man's children _____ thin and anemic.
   (become)

4. The aroma of sizzling meat _____ our mouths
   (make)
   water.

5. My brother _____ a big package home to Mother.
   (bring)

6. Although we were very poor, we never _____
   (steal)
   anything.

7. Father _____ to court after the rich man filed
   (go)
   a complaint.

8. The spectators _____ up when the judge entered
   (stand)
   the courtroom.

9. The judge _____ in his chair and pounded his gavel.
   (sit)

10. Father _____ all our coins and _____
    (take)   (put)
    them in a hat.

11. He _____ into the other room with his hat in his
    (stride)
    hands.

12. Saying, "Case dismissed," the judge _____ the
    (throw)
    case out.

13. After the trial, Father _____ hands with the judge.
    (shake)

14. The spectators _____ double with laughter when
    (bend)
    they _____ the rich man's complaint.
    (hear)

15. As we _____ older, we realized that money
    (grow)
    wasn't everything.

Exercise 2

In a group of three, make up a story. Write the story in the past tense. Each sentence in the story must contain a verb from the list. Verbs may be used more than once. Take turns adding a sentence. Continue the story until you have used all the verbs (or as many as you can). When you are finished, read your story to the class.

be	become	bring	come
eat	get	give	go
grow	have	join	keep
listen	live	look	pass
play	prefer	shake	sing
sit	sleep	stand	start
stay	stride	throw	watch
wonder			

Articles

*Fill in each blank with the definite article (*the*) or the indefinite article (*a or* an*).*

When I was four, I lived with my mother and brothers and sisters in _____ small town on _____ island of Luzon. We lived in
(1)   (2)

_____ town for several years. Father's farm had been destroyed in
(3)

1918 by _____ flood. We lived next door to _____ very rich man,
(4)   (5)

whose sons and daughters seldom came out of _____ house. While
(6)

we played in _____ sun, they stayed inside.
(7)

One of my brothers came home with _____ small bundle under
(8)

his arm, pretending that it was something good to eat, like _____
(9)

leg of lamb. He threw _____ bundle into Mother's lap. Suddenly
(10)

_____ black cat leaped out of _____ bundle and ran wildly
(11)   (12)

around _____ house. We laughed so hard that all our neighbors
(13)

except _____ rich family came into _____ yard and joined us.
(14)   (15)

FOLLOW UP

Topics for Discussion

1. Why was the rich man jealous of his poor neighbors instead of the other way around? Would you rather be in a family that was very poor but was happy or in a family that was very rich but not happy? Explain.

2. What could the rich man have learned from the poor family?

3. What are the negative results of being jealous? How can a person overcome feelings of jealousy?

4. Was anyone ever jealous of you? Describe how you handled the situation. Were you ever jealous of anyone? Describe how you handled that situation.

5. Have you ever had to go to court? Discuss the circumstances.

Topics for Writing

1. Being rich usually means having a great deal of money. In this story, however, the narrator says that his family was rich. Describe in a two-paragraph essay the ways in which you can be rich without having much money.

2. In a one-paragraph essay, describe a family you admire. What qualities do they possess?

3. Write a paragraph describing a special meal you cooked or ate. Use as many adjectives as you need to paint a clear picture of this meal. Some adjectives you might use are: delicious, sizzling, enchanting, tender, dripping, rare, soft, spicy, sweet, salty, crisp, sour, mouth-watering, and nourishing.

4. Have you ever had an argument with a neighbor or friend? What was it about? How did you settle it? Write a dialogue or short play presenting the situation.

5. In a two-paragraph essay, compare and contrast the rich man's children with the poor man's children.

Answer Key

Unit 1

Vocabulary

Vocabulary Builder
1. especially
2. excited
3. enough
4. use
5. confused
6. wonderful
7. large meal
8. design
9. terrible
10. accident
11. pay no attention to

Idiom Exercise

EXERCISE 1
1. jump to the conclusion
2. At worst, cut me out of his will
3. survive him

Word Forms
1. a. actor   c. acting
   b. act   d. Actions
2. a. invite   c. inviting
   b. invitation d. inviting
3. a. manage   c. management
   b. manager   d. managing
4. a. celebrating c. celebrity
   b. celebrate   d. celebration
5. a. amuse   c. amusement
   b. amusing   d. amusing

Structure

Verb Tenses: Simple Present and Past

EXERCISE 1

Every few days this month, I write another letter to Uncle Ben. But I never finish or mail these letters. I want to thank Uncle Ben for his Christmas present. But what is his present? I have no idea. I know one thing about this present: it is dangerous. Mr. Smither, the insurance adjuster, agrees with this. I know what the present isn't: it isn't a bean pot, a bed-warmer, a humidifier, or a barbecue. I show Uncle Ben's present to friends and ask them what it is, but no one seems to know. I hope Uncle Ben isn't angry at me!

Every few days this month, I wrote another letter to Uncle Ben. But I never finished or mailed these letters. I wanted to thank Uncle Ben for his Christmas present. But what was his present? I had no idea. I knew one thing about this present: it was dangerous. Mr. Smither, the insurance adjuster, agreed with this. I knew what the present wasn't: it wasn't a bean pot, a bed-warmer, a humidifier, or a barbecue. I showed Uncle Ben's present to friends and asked them what it was, but no one seemed to know. I hoped Uncle Ben wasn't angry at me!

EXERCISE 2

Maggie went (go) to the store and bought (buy) John a present. She sent (send) it to him by mail. After he received it, he wrote (write) her a thank-you letter. When she opened (open) it, she realized (realize) that he was thanking her for the wrong present. Obviously, John was (be) mixed up. Maggie wanted (want) to tell John about the mistake, but she was (be) afraid to embarrass him.

The next day, Maggie decided (decide) to prepare a birthday dinner for John. She made (make) a big pot of chicken and rice. The telephone rang (ring), and she forgot (forget) the food. It burned (burn) and exploded (explode). Maggie jumped (jump) from the noise.

When John came (come) to her house, she said, "I am (be) sorry. You forgot (forget) which gift I gave (give) you, and I forgot (forget) that I was cooking for your birthday."

Identifying Subjects and Verbs
1. We had
2. We received
3. present was
4. light dawned, it was
5. we can bake
6. We invited
7. feast is hissing
8. What caused
9. It is
10. Is this

155

Word Order: Statements

1. I managed to finish my letter.
2. Uncle Ben sent a lovely gift.
3. My friends often come to visit.
   (Or: Often my friends come to
   visit. My friends come to visit
   often.)
4. The pattern on this ceiling is
   very interesting.
5. Our insurance covers the cost
   of repainting the room.
6. John cleaned the carpet in the
   living room.
7. I should write a nice thank-you
   letter.
8. I decided to refinish the table.
9. She seemed very unhappy
   about something.
10. He gave each relative a gift.

Simple Present and Present Continuous

1. manage
2. is
3. is hissing
4. covers
5. suffer
6. is snoring
7. am writing
8. is
9. love
10. are staying
11. is washing, is shampooing
12. am waiting, am dashing

UNIT 2

Vocabulary

Vocabulary Builder

1. alert
2. hangover
3. abstinence
4. taste buds
5. habits
6. irritable
7. soothe
8. quitter
9. coward
10. willpower

Meanings of *So*

EXERCISE 1

1. c   2. a   3. d   4. b

Idiom Exercise

1. <u>Lay off</u> cigarettes if you want to
   stay healthy.
2. I can't <u>break the habit</u> of smoking.

3. My willpower <u>flew the coop</u>
   when I tried to break the
   smoking habit.
4. Most people eat more when
   they <u>kick the habit</u> of smoking.
5. If you are not careful, your bad
   habits will <u>come home to roost</u>.

Word Forms

1. a. irritating
   b. irritate
   c. irritable
   d. irritating
   e. irritation
2. a. hate
   b. Hating
   c. hateful
   d. Hatred
3. a. begin
   b. began
   c. beginner
   d. beginning
4. a. suggest
   b. suggestion
   c. suggesting
   d. suggested
5. a. master
   b. mastered
   c. masterful
   d. Mastering

Structure

Adjectives and Adverbs

EXERCISE 1

1. badly
2. honestly
3. easily
4. alertly
5. edgily
6. warmly
7. coldly
8. irritably
9. sharply
10. nervously

EXERCISE 2

1. bad
2. honest
3. easy
4. easily
5. alert
6. badly
7. nervous
8. warm
9. irritably
10. edgy
11. quickly

EXERCISE 4

Yesterday, I heard an <u>interesting</u>
story. It was about a student named
Norberto who was touring the
United States of America by bus. On
one of his tours, he sat next to a
<u>nervous</u> young man who smoked
many cigarettes. This made Norberto
<u>edgy</u> and <u>irritable.</u> Norberto asked
his neighbor to please stop smoking.
His neighbor replied, "I <u>honestly</u>
didn't know how my smoking
affected you. I shall stop so that you
can breathe <u>clean</u> air."

Norberto was so impressed by the
young man's kindness that he invited
him for lunch. Their friendship lasted
a <u>long</u> time.

Prepositions

EXERCISE 1

1. from
2. for
3. of
4. on
5. in
6. to, on, to
7. for
8. of
9. of
10. in

Some/Any

1. I didn't eat <u>any</u> sliced apples or
   quartered oranges for breakfast
   this morning.
2. The narrator doesn't want to
   eat <u>any</u> broccoli.
3. He didn't save <u>any</u> money last
   year when he stopped smoking.
4. The quitter didn't put on <u>any</u>
   weight this month.
5. Uncle Louis didn't want to
   knock <u>any</u> drinks out of
   people's hands.
6. Harriet didn't suggest that I
   take <u>any</u> baths.
7. I don't have to break <u>any</u> bad
   habits this year.
8. John didn't gain <u>any</u> weight
   after he stopped smoking.
9. I didn't run <u>any</u> errands for my
   wife.
10. I didn't smoke <u>any</u> cigarettes
    after dinner.

Grammatically Complete Sentences

1. Breakfast today was a sliced apple, a quartered orange, eight grapes, and raw carrots. (Or: For breakfast today I had a sliced apple, a quartered orange, eight grapes, and raw carrots.)
2. I take another warm bath.
3. I took two warm baths today.
4. I have coffee for breakfast. (Or: I drink coffee for breakfast.)
5. I discovered something interesting.
6. I didn't smoke cigarettes for a week.
7. I backed out of the garage.
8. I took a warm bath.
9. I had a cigarette hangover today.

Irregular Verbs: *To Be, To Do*, and *To Have*

1. is
2. are
3. am
4. does
5. is
6. Did
7. are
8. have
9. are
10. Do
11. Does
12. Do
13. have

Subject–Verb Agreement

1. makes
2. makes
3. remind
4. give
5. quit, get
6. has
7. notice, needs
8. is
9. have
10. makes, makes
11. make
12. do
13. does

Unit 3

Vocabulary

Vocabulary Builder

1. c	2. b	3. c	4. a
5. a	6. c	7. b	8. c
9. b	10. c	11. a	12. c

Idiom Exercise

1. b   2. c   3. a   4. c

Word Forms

1. a. applying
   b. apply
   c. application
2. a. appearance
   b. Appearing
   c. appear
   d. appeared

Structure

Some Confusing Subjects

1. is
2. are
3. is
4. meets
5. consists
6. does
7. are
8. interests
9. disagree
10. is

Word Order: Questions

1. What are my duties?
2. How much is the salary?
3. What kind of work is it?
4. Is there an opening here?
5. Do you think him odd?
6. May I ask who's calling?
7. Shouldn't I try to sell a piano?

Forming Questions

EXERCISE 1

1. Would you like to meet him?
2. What does the job pay?
3. Can you give me an idea?
4. What do you do all week?
5. Do you want to meet the manager?
6. Do you take the pianos out?
7. Whom are you married to?

Exercise 2

1. What is Newbegin's?
2. Is Newbegin's in San Francisco?
3. Do you like being among the pianos?
4. Can you tell me what my duties are?
5. What is the salary?
6. What is your ambition?

Present Perfect Tense

1. have worked
2. has tuned
3. has urged
4. have scribbled
5. Have (you) looked
6. have decided

7. Have (you) located
8. has worn
9. has told
10. have kept, have (ever) made
11. have known
12. has (already) gotten
13. has kept
14. Have (they) raised
15. Have (you) gotten

Past Tense

1. was
2. had, went
3. married
4. left, was
5. applied
6. told
7. quit
8. became
9. asked
10. introduced, asked
11. examined
12. walked
13. entered, saw
14. sat
15. found
16. decided
17. thought
18. called
19. made
20. folded, held

Unit 4

Vocabulary

Vocabulary Builder

1. not locked
2. friend
3. introduced
4. leave out
5. show
6. hurt
7. family

Structure

Sentence Combining

EXERCISE 1

1. I picked up my check and went home.
2. Saturday I went to the personnel department, and the girl there said, "I've got an exciting position to offer you."
3. She offered me the sporting goods job, but I wasn't interested in it.
4. Anyone can come into the warehouse now, but no one comes.

5. It's nice of you to say I'm famous, but hardly anybody knows me.
6. I took my lunch and ate it under the ramp of the bridge.
7. I didn't get killed in Korea, but I did get wounded.
8. No one is here, but someone might arrive soon.
9. I walked around the desk and put my hand out, and we shook hands.
10. I took her in my arms and kissed her.
11. I tried to be businesslike, but couldn't.
12. I heard Mr. Spezzafly coming, but I couldn't stop kissing Stella.
13. He left the office, and Stella and I listened to him walking back to his office.
14. She started crying, and I did, too.

EXERCISE 2
1. I went to my office, and I sat at my desk.
2. The girl in the blue dress stepped up to my desk, and she held out a piece of folded paper to me.
3. Stella seemed brave, but I was scared.
4. I hardly know you, but / yet I know you're famous.
5. I eat my lunch in the park, for I enjoy the fresh air.
6. I didn't leave my office at twelve o'clock, so I had no lunch.
7. I didn't have a token, so I didn't take the subway.
8. I left my job two months ago, but the checks are still coming.
9. I can go to work, or I can stay home.
10. I can go to your house, or you can come to mine.

Capitalization

There wasn't a visitor all week. Friday afternoon I picked up my check and went home, and Saturday morning I went up to the personnel department again, and the girl there said, "I've got a rather exciting position to offer you in the sporting goods department. Mr. Plattock wants a likely-looking man to demonstrate the rowing machine and the limbering-up bicycle. Would you like to meet Mr. Plattock?"

Monday I took my lunch and ate it under the Fremont Street ramp of the Bay Bridge, while Mr. Spezzafly ate his at his desk.

I think about when I was eighteen and got in the Marines and went to Korea and got wounded and got discharged in San Francisco.

Future Tense

EXERCISE 1
1. Clewpor is going to be married.
2. Spezzafly is going to open the warehouse door.
3. Stella is going to look for a job.
4. Ashland is going to tell her about his childhood.
5. The personnel director is going to offer Ashland a new job.
6. The baby is going to be famous.
7. No one is going to buy any pianos.
8. I am going to move the pianos again.
9. Clewpor is going to call Mr. Spezzafly on the telephone.
10. The personnel manager is going to offer him several jobs.
11. Clewpor is going to refuse most of them.
12. He is going to prefer to stay with Mr. Spezzafly.
13. Clewpor is going to ask Stella to marry him.
14. They are going to spend a great deal of money on their new house.
15. He is going to pick me up on the way to the office.

EXERCISE 2
1. You'll make an excellent impression.
2. If you say, "Visitor in the warehouse," I'll understand what you're telling me.
3. Will you visit the warehouse?
4. You'll find the door unlocked.
5. If someone comes in, I'll let you know.
6. He won't leave Mr. Spezzafly.
7. His baby will be famous.

Verb Tense Review
1. was
2. lived
3. adopted
4. ran
5. joined
6. fought
7. thinks
8. died
9. works
10. talks
11. wants
12. feels
13. is beginning
14. is making
15. are waiting
16. has
17. is
18. will marry / is going to marry
19. will buy / is going to buy
20. will have / are going to have
21. will be / are going to be

Word Order: Place and Time
1. Clewpor met Stella for lunch at a fancy restaurant on Tuesday.
2. Mr. Spezzafly left the warehouse a few minutes ago.
3. Mr. Spezzafly spoke on the telephone in his office on Tuesday.
4. We unlatched the door to the warehouse yesterday.
5. Ashland and Stella went to a concert on Thursday night.
6. That fellow goes to work with me on the subway every morning.
7. Ashland receives a visitor in his office every week.
8. Stella does her typing in the office every Monday.
9. Mr. Spezzafly checks the pianos at the warehouse once a month.
10. Ashland kissed Stella in the office last week.

UNIT 5

Vocabulary

Vocabulary Builder
1. lining
2. parcels
3. plunged
4. protested
5. trampled
6. savagely
7. swearing
8. tail
9. peculiar
10. grunt, exultation

Idiom Exercise
1. c   2. a   3. d
4. b   5. b

Word Forms

1. a. borrow
   b. borrower
   c. borrowing
2. a. assuring
   b. assurance
   c. assured
3. a. obligation
   b. obligatory
   c. oblige
   d. obliging

Structure

This/That; These/Those

1. those
2. these
3. this
4. this, these
5. That
6. That
7. those
8. this
9. That

There is/There are

1. are
2. is
3. Are
4. is
5. is

Possessive Pronouns

1. ours
2. mine
3. His, his
4. his
5. his
6. theirs
7. mine
8. ours
9. theirs
10. mine

Present Continuous

1. He is wearing a dark suit.
2. He is walking in the park now.
3. He is carrying a walking stick in his right hand now.
4. He is borrowing matches from his friends now.
5. He is taking the trouble to help a stranger.
6. He is bringing his son candy.
7. The tailor is calling me to come in for a fitting.
8. I am trying to quit smoking.
9. My son is taking things from my pockets.
10. I am looking for matches in my jacket pockets.

Quotation Marks

As I was walking down the street on a very cold snowy night, a man approached me and said, "Could you please give me a match?"

I looked at the man carefully. He was wearing black pants, a black hat, and black gloves. Something about him frightened me. Again he asked me to give him a match. As I reached into my pocket, he said, "Please hurry. I'm very cold."

"I'm doing the best I can," I answered. My hands were shaking. I wanted to tell him that I had no matches. However, I set my teeth, reached into my pocket, and gave him my lighter.

After he lit his cigarette, he returned my lighter and said with a smile, "Thank you. I was afraid to ask a stranger for a match, but I wanted to smoke so badly that I overcame my fears. Have a good evening."

Expressing Uncertainty

1. I think I have a match.
2. I guess it may be in the top pocket.
3. There must be one in here somewhere.
4. I guess it must be in with my watch.
5. I think it's in my hip pocket.
6. I guess it could be in the bottom pocket.
7. It might be in the overcoat lining.

UNIT 6

Comprehension

1. c	2. a	3. a	4. b
5. a	6. a	7. b	

Vocabulary

Vocabulary Builder

1. no
2. no
3. no
4. yes
5. yes
6. no
7. no
8. no
9. yes
10. no

Structure

Prepositions

EXERCISE 1

1. at
2. on
3. of
4. with
5. in
6. of
7. in
8. with
9. into
10. behind
11. out

Contractions

1. What's
2. Can't
3. don't
4. she'd
5. wasn't
6. We're
7. I'm
8. Let's
9. wouldn't
10. They'll
11. I'm
12. You've

Past Continuous Tense

EXERCISE 1

1. was sitting
2. was not hurting / wasn't hurting
3. was visualizing
4. was talking
5. was undressing
6. was holding

EXERCISE 2

1. was talking
2. turned
3. saw
4. was holding
5. was driving
6. slowed
7. sighed
8. came
9. saw
10. was walking
11. was trying

Past Perfect Tense

1. had been, had not done
2. had sat
3. had turned, had gone
4. had stopped
5. had stopped
6. had filed

7. had remarried
8. had driven
9. had hurt
10. had told

Adjectives and Adverbs
(Other answers are possible.)
1. Mrs. Bidwell looked at him penetratingly.
2. The car stopped despondently.
3. Mrs. Bidwell slept soundly.
4. "Hawwwwww," Mr. Bidwell would say, in a thick voice.
5. Mr. Bidwell's heart lifted slightly.
6. She stood in a quiet way behind his chair.
7. He tried to let out his breath in an imperceptible way.
8. "I see you," she said coldly.
9. Everything went smoothly for a month or so.
10. He looked at her venomously.

Would in Past Time
EXERCISE 1

Mrs. Bidwell, ordinarily a sound sleeper, would wake up and shake her husband. "George!" she would say.

"Hawwwwww," Mr. Bidwell would say, thickly. "Wahs maa nah, hm?"

After he had turned over and gone back to sleep, Mrs. Bidwell would lie awake, thinking.

UNIT 7

Vocabulary
Vocabulary Builder
1. glutton
2. core, gulp
3. rim
4. adapted
5. affection
6. bin
7. leap
8. dawn
9. skull
10. gradually

Word Forms
1. a. decisive
   b. decision
   c. deciding
   d. decide
2. a. wasteful
   b. waste
   c. wasting
3. a. discovery
   b. discover
   c. discovering

4. a. refusal
   b. refused
   c. refusing
5. a. cooperation
   b. cooperate
   c. cooperative
   d. cooperating

Structure
Adjectives and Adverbs
1. great
2. brooding
3. trusting
4. baleful
5. sharply
6. prodigious
7. Suddenly
8. ludicrous
9. obviously
10. large
11. eagerly
12. simple
13. gradually

Comparatives and Superlatives of Adjectives
EXERCISE 1
1. freshest
2. most baleful
3. hungriest
4. hungrier
5. bigger
6. larger
7. most gigantic
8. closer
9. higher
10. closest
11. swiftest
12. heavier
13. happier

Pronouns and Reflexive Pronouns
EXERCISE 1
1. Henry Pludge had a foolproof plan to win the fishing derby. It was ludicrously simple. He decided that he would catch a salmon, keep it alive in a tank in his basement, fatten it up for a year, and walk away with the first prize.
2. Henry built a large steel tank in his basement, swore his wife to secrecy, and went fishing.
3. It was only in the spring that Sam appeared unhappy, and the sound of him leaping and slapping the surface kept the Pludges awake many nights. Once, they had to go down

and carry him back to the tank from the sawdust bin where a prodigious leap had carried him.
EXERCISE 2
1. it
2. himself, it
3. himself
4. him
5. himself
6. him
7. him
8. him
9. him
10. himself

UNIT 8

Vocabulary
Vocabulary Builder
1. junk
2. invention, patented
3. gadget
4. magical
5. absorb
6. aptitude
7. rapid
8. conceivable
9. drawback
10. initial

Idiom Exercise
1. catching on
2. being brought up on
3. at will
4. making an appearance

Word Forms
EXERCISE 1
1. a. magician
   b. magical
   c. magic
2. a. build
   b. builder, built
   c. building
3. a. teacher
   b. teach
   c. teaching
4. a. comfortable
   b. comforting
   c. comfort
5. a. inform
   b. informative
   c. information

Exercise 2
1. accessory
2. armchair
3. backward
4. basically
5. bookmark
6. drawback
7. electronic
8. entirely
9. ingenious
10. information
11. learning
12. magical
13. nothing
14. nowadays
15. revolutionary

Structure

Subject–Verb Agreement
1. Indications <u>are</u> that if it catches on, all the electronic gadgets will be so much junk.
2. Many <u>advantages</u> <u>are</u> claimed over the old-style learning and teaching aids on which most *people* are brought up nowadays.
3. Each <u>sheet</u> <u>bears</u> a number of sequence, so that the sheets cannot be used in the wrong order.
4. Each <u>sheet</u> of paper <u>presents</u> the user with an information sequence in the form of symbols, which <u>he</u> absorbs optically for automatic registration on the brain.
5. When one <u>sheet</u> <u>has</u> been assimilated, a mere <u>flick</u> of the finger turns it over and further <u>information</u> is found on the other side.
6. By using both sides of each sheet in this way, a great <u>economy</u> <u>is</u> effected.
7. No <u>buttons</u> <u>need</u> to be pressed to move from one sheet to another.
8. <u>Nothing</u> <u>has</u> to be connected up or switched on.
9. The user may turn at will to any sheet, going backward or forward as <u>he</u> <u>pleases</u>.
10. A small <u>accessory,</u> available at trifling extra cost, <u>is</u> the bookmark.
11. The motive <u>power,</u> thanks to the ingenious device patented by the makers, <u>is</u> supplied by the brain of the user.

Active and Passive Sentences
1. BOOK can be used by anyone.
2. Many advantages are claimed.
3. It can be used conveniently.
4. A great economy is effected.
5. A great future is predicted for it.
6. The information is absorbed by the user.
7. The ingenious device was patented by the makers.
8. An information sequence is presented by each sheet.
9. The sheets are held by a special locking device.
10. BOOKmark may be used in any book.
11. Electronic gadgets will be replaced by BOOK.

Phrasal Verbs
Exercise 1
1. connected up, break down
2. switched on
3. turn to
4. pick up, left off
5. catches on

Unit 9

Vocabulary

Vocabulary Builder
Exercise 1
1. yes
2. no
3. no
4. no
5. no
6. no
7. no
8. no
9. yes
10. no
11. yes
12. yes

Idiom Exercise
1. weighted down with
2. broke into tears
3. to smooth things over
4. sick to my stomach
5. came to her aid
6. stop by

Prefixes and Suffixes
Exercise 1
1. false
2. true
3. true

4. false
5. true
6. true
7. false
Exercise 2
1. a, c, e, g
2. b, c, d, e
3. a, c, e, g
4. a, c, e, g

Understanding Drug Labels
Exercise 1
1. side effects
2. symptom
3. prescription
4. warning
5. doses
6. refill
Exercise 2
1. Anna Fields
2. One teaspoon
3. four
4. Dr. Pillsbury
5. zero
Exercise 3
1. No-Cold Cherry Lozenges
2. minor sore-throat pain
3. one lozenge
4. every two hours (every three hours for children)
5. eight (four for children)
6. sore throat that lasts more than two days; high fever, headache, nausea, or vomiting
7. User should not give lozenges to children under six unless directed by physician.

To Make
(Other answers are possible.)
1. draw
2. manufacture
3. construct
4. knit
5. bake
6. be
7. brand
8. schedule
9. total
10. earn
11. divide
12. give
13. arrange
14. cook

Structure

Cloze Exercise
1. the
2. a
3. told
4. admire
5. live
6. take
7. always
8. for
9. We're
10. of
11. don't

The Pronoun *It*
1. Heventizeall
2. just the thing for an upset stomach
3. allergy
4. take the Egazzakine
5. not being able to move the arm
6. something to take if not able to move the arm
7. doesn't refer
8. that the sore throat is back

Direct and Indirect Objects
EXERCISE 1
1. You don't take <u>pills.</u>
2. I have just the <u>thing</u> for (you)
3. Heventizeall doesn't make <u>you</u> sleepy.
4. I have a <u>bottle</u> at the hotel.
5. I'll give (you) some <u>pills.</u>
6. I no longer had my <u>sore throat.</u>
7. I couldn't eat the <u>food.</u>
8. I ran into an American <u>friend.</u>
9. He recognized the <u>symptoms.</u>
10. I reported <u>this</u> to my (friend.)
11. The doctor gave (me) <u>something.</u>
12. I'll send <u>it</u> to (you)
13. I didn't mention <u>it</u> to a (soul.)

EXERCISE 2
1. I'll give you some.
2. cannot be rewritten
3. The doctor gave something to me.
4. cannot be rewritten
5. I'll send you it.
6. cannot be rewritten
7. I'll give the medicine to you.
8. He offered them to me.

UNIT 10

Vocabulary

Vocabulary Builder
EXERCISE 1
1. gavel
2. strutted
3. spirit
4. aroma, wafted, gratuitously
5. wrestled
6. undo
7. sizzling
8. sturdy
9. contagious, spectators
10. complexion
11. several, proceed
12. herd
13. grotesque
14. glowered

Structure

Irregular Verbs—Past Tense
1. sang
2. came
3. became
4. made
5. brought
6. stole
7. went
8. stood
9. sat
10. took, put
11. strode
12. threw
13. shook
14. bent, heard
15. grew

Articles
1. a
2. the
3. the
4. a
5. a
6. the
7. the
8. a
9. a
10. the
11. a
12. the
13. the
14. the
15. the

Copyrights and Acknowledgments

Laugh And Learn

Felder

| Name | date |

Laugh and Learn

Humorous American Short Stories

Second Edition

Mira B. Felder / Anna Bryks Bromberg

Humorous American short stories from classic writers such as William Saroyan, James Thurber, Art Buchwald, Maggie Grant, Jack Scott, and more— all **unadapted and unabridged!**

These beguiling stories offer **intermediate** students a positive introduction to American literature, life, and culture. Because exercises encourage students to relate their own experiences to the stories, they will be motivated to read more, speak more, and write more.

Features:

- Pre- and post-reading activities and generous, clear glossing make these stories accessible to intermediate students.
- Follow-up activities provide extensive practice with vocabulary, idioms, and grammar.

Other literature-based readers from Addison Wesley Longman:

Addison
Wesley
Longman

 LONGMAN

90000

9 780201 834147

ISBN 0-201-83414-6

If I Were a Fish

Written by Susan Caver

Illustrated by Darcia Labrosse